THE LUMINOUS SEA

THE
LUMINOUS

SEA

MELISSA BARBEAU

BREAKWATER
P.O. Box 2188, St. John's, NL, Canada, A1C 6E6
www.breakwaterbooks.com

LIBRARY AND ARCHIVES CANADA CATALOGUING IN PUBLICATION
Barbeau, Melissa, author
The luminous sea / Melissa Barbeau.
ISBN 978-1-55081-737-9 (softcover)
I. Title.
PS8603.A704L86 2018   C813'.6   C2018-900350-2

We acknowledge the support of the Canada Council for the Arts, which last year
invested $153 million to bring the arts to Canadians throughout the country.
We acknowledge the financial support of the Government of Canada and the
Government of Newfoundland and Labrador through the Department of Tourism,
Culture, Industry and Innovation for our publishing activities.
PRINTED AND BOUND IN CANADA.

Canada Council
for the Arts

Conseil des Arts
du Canada

Canadä

Newfoundland
Labrador

Breakwater Books is committed to choosing papers and materials for our books that
help to protect our environment. To this end, this book is printed on a recycled paper
that is certified by the Forest Stewardship Council®.

For Freshwater
And all the people I love that end up there

AT SEA

THE night air is warm on the luminous sea. Water laps against the hull. There is a splash as something unseen breaches the surface of the bay and Vivienne glances overboard. The air smells of brine and bilge water. Land smells drift on the breeze—smoke from dying fires that glow like lighted matches on the far beaches, hay meadows, the smell of the woods. A fragranced world made of base notes and top notes, scents you notice right away and ones that come later, that linger. Like perfume. There are land sounds, too, but they are far away and miniature. Splinters of laughter, the heartbeat bass thrum of a radio heard as if through a thick pane of glass, fading as night shuffles its way towards dawn.

The punt cuts a slow swath through a cloud of phosphorescence. Vivienne stops long enough to make a note on a chart—dinoflagellates—letting the engine idle. Overhead, the moon is blue. She turns towards it, her face illuminated in its light. She has heard the phrase before, of course. *Once in a blue moon.* Hardly never, that's what it means. Which is just about how often she hears from Eliza, how often the old Evinrude starts on the first pull and she doesn't just about yank her shoulder out of its socket trying to get it going, how often they see a whale in this bay anymore.

But tonight it is literal. The moon is blue, at least from the perspective of the boat bobbing on the quiet sea. Vivienne tries to classify it, to imagine where it falls on the colour spectrum. Somewhere closer to green than purple. Turquoise with some kind of sheen to it. A trick of atmospheric pressure or space dust or smog or some kind of emissions in the upper stratosphere. A fish scale in the sky.

Whatever has caused it, there it hangs, swollen and pregnant, the reflected light staining the air and the water and the little boat. Saturating everything in the bay with colour, even Vivienne herself, as if a blue gel has been fitted over the moon, as if she is in a movie.

She has been in Damson Bay all summer, collecting samples, taking measurements. She has spent most of her time waiting. Waiting on permits and waiting for the weather to cooperate. Waiting on phone calls that never come. Waiting on shore while the wind blows and the surf pounds the landwash, whole weeks wasted to summer storms. Waiting for nights and days when there isn't a lop on the water. Waiting for the sea to be lopless.

She has spent the first part of this early morning excursion putting around the cove, nosing in and around the slipway and the pilings of the dock, and along the slippery rocks at the end of the beach. Leaning overboard with a thermometer to take water temperature, scooping samples from the swaths of jellyfish choking the harbour. Now she is out of the shelter of the cove and has rounded the corner into the wider bay. She pulls in close to the granite cliff face and cuts the engine. The boat drifts in the current on a lethargic collision course with the escarpment. The ocean world beneath the keel beneath her feet is weird and fantastic. She shines a flashlight into the water. The beam catches crabs scuttling between waving fronds of seaweed. Flatfish swim toward the light.

Vivienne dips up jellyfish and weighs them and records the size of them and the number and the type on a laminated chart with a waterproof pencil crayon before tipping most of them back into the sea. Some she drops into plastic containers filled with seawater, the location pencilled on the lids, before navigating to the next location to do the same thing over again. Her eyes grow accustomed to the dark even as the first hint of sunrise warms the horizon. Domed jellyfish with trailing tentacles and sea gooseberries with runways of fluorescent lights stretching the length of them, illuminating as they feed, pulse their way through the water. Vivienne retrieves a handline from the bottom of the boat and casts the jigger overboard, watching the bottle-green line unspool. The barb hooks a pair of opalescent bodies as it rockets to the sea floor, dragging them into the depths.

The fishermen in the cove had given her warning way back in June, after spying the lead fishing lure staring sightlessly from the bottom of the boat, that it was weeks before the food fishery opened. Admonishing her about the local DFO officer, describing her down to her caterpillar eyebrows.

They told her stories of impounded boats, of trailers and trucks confiscated right on the beach, but their expressions had changed when she'd shown them the sampling permit she'd finally been issued, the one that said she had permission to fish out of season and as much as she wanted. She'd pulled it out to reassure them, waving it around in the plastic Ziploc baggie she'd put it in to keep it dry, jabbering about sampling jellyfish predators if she could find them. She'd started to ask about some of the bigger apex species up here—sea turtles and tuna—when she realized she was over her head in silence. Her voice trailed off as she asked if they ever saw sharks and someone said we sure do. The silence fathoms deep and she'd fallen into it, or maybe she'd been pushed.

Still, there were words of caution and advice when she said she planned to go out by herself. Shaking their heads at the thought of her alone on the water at night.

Vivienne turns the wooden spindle of the jigger in lazy circles. The bottom feels a long way down, the boat has drifted off the marks while she gazed up foolish at the moon. She pulls at the fishing line, a slow steady back and forth. Tedium and meditation. A summer's worth of jigging has worn the paint from the edge of the wave-weathered gunwale. Vivienne feels something tug at the line and starts to pull, hand over hand, until she feels the line slacken. She keeps pulling, knowing a fish will sometimes swim up with the line. Two more times, left hand over right, and the line goes taut again. The weight of it. A big cod or maybe even the porbeagle she'd heard was in the cove. Bold enough to swim up and take a fish right off a line, fishermen pulling up a cod and the bottom of it bitten clean off. Her hands start to ache and the pain that has lurked in her back for the past two weeks bites her sharply between the shoulder blades. A shape emerges, it looms into focus as it nears the surface of the water, and the sight of it makes Vivienne's breath catch in her throat like a barb and there is an instant where the line snags against the oarlock and she thinks she will lose her grip but she gives a final heave and pulls her catch up and over the side and right into the plastic fish box in the bottom of the boat.

The creature is longer than the fish box and lean, her flukes draping over the edge, seaweed dripping from her shoulders. Vivienne thinks the fish will pull herself over the side of the boat and launch herself back into the water but she has been hooked through the cheek and as she thrashes the line tangles itself around her kelp-strewn torso and it is only moments, it seems, and she is gasping and still in the bottom of the boat.

Vivienne picks up the ice-cream bucket she uses for bailing and leans overboard to scoop enough seawater to fill the fish box a couple of inches. Reverse bailing. The creature pushes one side of her gilled face into the puddle of water, gasping for breath. She lies on the hook embedded in her face and as she struggles to breathe it presses more deeply into her flesh. Petals of red bloom from beneath her cheek suffusing the water with colour. Vivienne thinks it is like watching a teabag stain the water in a cup of tea when you press on it with a spoon and she wonders what would happen if she pressed down the same way with her foot on the creature's face.

The air is warm. The sea is luminous. A tremor ricochets through the creature's body and then she is motionless.

Vivienne thinks she cannot be conscious. She wonders if she can breathe. For one moment, for one single breath, while the boat barely rocks on the glowing sea, Vivienne imagines easing the barbed jigger from the creature's face. She imagines pouring the fish out of the fish box into the sea in a waterfall of red, the red fading to pink and then to nothingness in the endless wash of waves. Vivienne imagines the creature swimming away, slapping her tail on the water, but before the fish can disappear beneath the waves the fantasy vanishes.

Instead, Vivienne's mind leaps ahead to the moment she will bump the boat up to the dock, and she clicks into emergency mode, as if she is at the scene of an accident, or a helicopter crash. Her disembodied hands pulse in anticipation as they await instructions from her brain. She is ready to assess damage, triage, check for vital signs, apply pressure. She imagines who might be waiting at the wharf and she searches the bottom of the boat for anything she might use to conceal the creature. Piles a cast net on top of her, fluffing it up as if it is a down duvet. Tucks the creature in with her slicker, not quite hospital corners, but almost, and then lays her head on the bundle and listens. Nothing. She pokes at the pile with her finger and jumps back when she feels the creature jerk. The boat rocks beneath her feet. She takes off her hoodie and adds it to the heap, like clothes thrown haphazardly, casually, on a perfectly made bed.

It takes three tries to turn over the outboard motor. By the time Vivienne pulls alongside the wharf the water in the fish box will be opaque and it will be impossible to see the bottom of it.

SEEN

I T is the kind of glassy night when sound travels miles across the surface of the sea; the air a crystal wineglass, susceptible to the slightest flick of a fingertip. The kind of night you might hear the sigh of lovers on the breeze, or the sound of a last breath.

From the punt a person watching out over the bay—someone sitting on a tumble-down rock wall marking the outlines of a vanished garden at the top of the hill—is impossible to see. A spot of black on a field of darkness. Hidden in plain view.

There is no such thing as a secret in a small town. Nothing goes unnoticed. Tip the salt shaker over on the kitchen table and the next morning someone in line at the post office will ask if you remembered to throw a pinch over your left shoulder to shoo away the Devil.

MEET TAMA

THE movement of the knife is quick and definite, the woman's hand sure. Tama grabs a fleshy dome from a bowl, slices it into strips, and tosses the strips into a plastic tub sitting at her elbow on the stainless steel counter; the tub filling with every handful added, cellophane ribbons sliding over one another like worms. The knife thunks, the little hill of wet flesh grows, dripping and slippery. The pile of whole jellyfish shrinking until all that is left in the bottom of the bowl is a milky sludge.

The knife is razor sharp and an indulgence. A true chef's knife, not something you can save up stamps for at the grocery store. Bradley had ordered it for Tama online. He had meant it to be symbolic, as well as practical: to show how seriously they are taking this new endeavour, this move to Damson Bay. To show that they intend to approach the little bistro they have opened as a *quality project*, that they have some idea what they are up to, that they are intent on the whole thing. Tama supposes, too, that she is meant to understand they are severing old ties and slicing away at bad habits, that they are starting over new.

The fluorescent lights glare off the window in front of her, obscuring the outside world. From the radio peal twangy guitars. The country channel is the only station that will hold tune out here, and in the pre-dawn hour, before the morning-show host has signed on, it is all old songs about heartbreak and loss. The signal is clear as a bell. On the other side of the kitchen window she can't see out of, the sky must be cloudless.

A stockpot of brine, and another filled with Mason jars, bubble on the stove. A handful of lids dance next to them in a saucepan of boiling water. Tama snaps the lid from a Tupperware container. The tub is filled with oak leaves. The smell of chlorophyll wafts out.

Despite the new knife the café is not even close to breaking even. Tama has installed a shelf next to the cash register which she has stocked with preserves of all kinds—jams and marmalades and mussels in brine—hoping to generate a little extra revenue. She has taken a chance with the jellyfish.

The fishermen stopping in for a cup of coffee after coming off the water offer ever more apocalyptic opinions about the jellyfish blooms smothering the coastline: they're getting so thick, maid, the boat brings up short on them; the bay's going to be a bowl of gelatine, mix in a little custard and you'll have dessert; I believe they must go all the way down— won't be long now you'll be able to jump off the cliff by the lighthouse and bounce your way over to the far point.

But to Tama, the conversations had brought to mind the

jellyfish salads she had first eaten in a Japanese restaurant in Paris. The summer Bradley never made it over for a visit because he wanted to row in the St. John's Regatta. Strips of jellyfish and ginger and chili flakes. A glass of chilled saké. The dish had been unexpectedly perfect for a muggy August evening on the Left Bank. She had Googled "preserving jellyfish" and found a recipe that used oak leaves instead of some unpronounceable chemical preservative to keep them from losing their crunch, so she marked "all-natural" on the labels and they had proved to be a surprising hit. Although maybe not so surprising in a town that still hosts an annual seal flipper dinner or where you might find a drop of fish head stew bubbling away on someone's stove on any old Friday evening.

She picked the leaves from the trees that hemmed in the overgrown gardens of the grand turn-of-the-century house crowning the hill that rimmed Damson Bay. The house had been built by a local shipbuilder. When Tama was a girl it had overlooked the harbour—the structure grey and imperious—but in the years she had been away, the house had burned to the ground. The trees still stood, gnarled and cantankerous-looking. The garden was a good place to be if you were feeling a little bent and crooked and cantankerous yourself.

Earlier in the day she had climbed onto the lower branches of one of the ancient oaks, and had a lunch of crackers and cheese and a thermos of tea, her feet swinging. Her eyes following the trail down the hill and along the beach until it disappeared from sight, though she knew it kept going out into the country where her father had once set his rabbit snares. She followed it back to the crumbling lighthouse on the point, and then past the point into the bay. The tide was on its way out. The stacks of a sunken ship were visible, the decks slowly revealed, exposing a garden of kelp. From her roost Tama spotted a green pickup truck as it pulled away from the building the crowd from the university had rented for the summer. It bounced along the gravel road and into the centre of town, stopping in the parking lot of the café. She had watched as a figure stepped out of the cab. Then monkeyed her way down the branches and headed back down the hill.

Tama rescues the bottles on the stove with a long set of tongs and adds a layer of leaves to each one. She fills each one with a ladleful of fleshy ribbons and tops them with boiling brine. Screws the lids on tight. When a line of jelly jars filled with jellyfish lines the back counter she pours a glass of gin. Opens the screen door and steps outside to wait for dawn to peep its way into the bay.

The world is glowing—the moon, the stars. The sea. Light spills from the windows of the glorified lab across the bay. Dew collects on the deck. Tama looks for the green pickup truck and, as if she's wished it out of hiding, the truck rumbles into sight and heads for the wharf. She cannot see inside the cab. The truck pulls to a stop and a single person gets out and leans against the bonnet, looking out over the water. Tama watches long enough to decide no one else is getting out of the truck. No one is waiting in the cab. Her arms are cold, she has not brought a sweater. Her glass is empty. She hears an outboard motor. A boat heading in the bay. She doesn't stay long enough to see it dock or to watch the sun come up.

LANDING

THE boat, Vivienne knows, will be heard before it is seen, the sound of the motor amplified in the early morning quiet.

The trick will be to pull in without drawing attention. The trick will be to take her time. Vivienne lets the outboard putt along—the wake churning like cream as it's whipped, or like eggs when she makes meringue. Not frenzied, just folding over itself. She is moseying in the cove as if she is in no hurry at all. As if she has all the time in the world. She hopes Thomas isn't hanging around the wharf. Or Bradley. Or anyone else propped up on their elbows on the breakwater or sitting in a truck smoking until the air in the cab turns so blue she wonders how they manage to see out the windshield.

But as she pulls into sight of the dock there is only the green truck and only Colleen pushing a foot off the bumper. No firefly pricks of light signalling lit cigarettes. No elbows holding heads up on the breakwater, no smoke-filled cabs. No Bradley riding shotgun. Vivienne casts a quick glance towards the light pole. No ATV parked there. No Thomas.

The dock is close enough now that Vivienne can see the chipping yellow paint, the slimy concrete slipway, the oxidized mooring cleats. She lets go of the throttle and cuts the engine. The boat drifts the last few feet, bumping against the creosote-soaked wood. Colleen waits for Vivienne to pull close enough to toss her the painter. Vivienne throws it but the throw is short and it bounces off a tire bolted to the side of the wharf and into the water. She reels it in again, her hands wet and raw, while Colleen frowns with impatience. Annoyed to be wasting time on Vivienne's foolishness. Vivienne tries again, and this time Colleen catches the rope with her big hands, looping it around the iron cleat, securing it with a strangling bowline. Vivienne's heart hammers, her fingers like claws, frozen into the shape of the outboard motor's grip.

"How'd you make out?"

Vivienne says nothing. Shakes her head.

"Get all five buckets filled? You were awfully quick."

Nothing.

"You know everything needs to be done to spec. We can't have skewed results because of lazy data collection."

Vivienne picks up one of the filled sample buckets, trying to clear things out of the way, but it slips from her grasp. Her nervousness is palpable. She loses her balance and falls forward, hitting the side of her face on the gunwale. She drops the bucket and water sloshes out of it. She can feel a bump rise on her cheekbone.

"Jesus, Viv, watch what you're doing."

"We're in a hurry tonight, Colleen. I think we have to hurry."

"What are you on about? Who's waiting for you? That Tom? Are you in that much of a hurry to meet up with that Tom? I didn't think he was your type."

"The fish box, Colleen. Help me with the fish box."

Vivienne is moving quickly, recklessly around the boat, rushing. The boat is rocking precariously.

"The buckets first, girl, or we'll never get at the fish box."

Vivienne sees the sense of this and starts handing up plastic pails. Colleen reaches down for them, one at a time, and saunters over to the truck with them. Slides them to the back of the pan. Saunters her way back. She is taking it slow and easy. On the return trips she pushes her hands into her pockets.

"Please, Colleen. Please. Grab the end of the box. We have to get it up into the truck." The pitch of Vivienne's voice is rising like an opera singer's warm-up arpeggios, sliding up the scale like something you'd hear in the afternoon on the CBC. Vivienne is beginning to feel disembodied. She wonders if she might teleport herself out of this situation if she only thinks it hard enough. Teleport herself away from Colleen and the need to get the fish box and its fishy cargo out of the boat and into the pan of the truck before anyone pulls onto the apron of the wharf.

She can hear the whine of a quad.

"Colleen. I need you to take the end. It's too heavy for me." Vivienne is crashing around inside the bottom of the boat now like a bull in a china shop or a bear in a boat. A clumsy no-thumbed bear unable to get a grip on anything: the fish box, reality. She is kicking at the spool of the jigger, tripping in the line, falling over the seat.

"I have something. I have something in here. We need to get her out of here. We need to get her into the truck."

"What? What have you got in there?" Colleen's interest is finally peaked. "What's in there?"

Colleen jumps into the boat and throws aside the sweatshirt Vivienne has draped across the made bed with its almost-hospital corners. The outline of the creature's tail obvious beneath the creased yellow slicker. The ATV is coming closer. It is making its way down the hill path, the bumpy road making the headlights jump. There is a small movement beneath the gear. There is a monster in the bed. Colleen snatches her hand away.

"It's alive." A statement, not a question.

It's alive. Vivienne feels a whoosh of blood to her heart.

"Please." Vivienne is pleading. She tries to find a seam of excitement lacing the fear racing through her circulatory system, but it is nowhere to be found. Instead, she feels nauseated. She urges a little.

Colleen comprehends, finally, the gravity of the situation.

"Get it together," she snaps.

The weight of her discovery is pressing down on Vivienne's shoulders, the weight of discovery and the fear that she is murdering this thing, that the creature is drowning in the bloody bottom of the box. She pictures again the hook through the cheek, the lead jigger dangling from the wound.

But things move quickly then. Colleen jumps out of the boat barking instructions. They heave, Vivienne in the boat and Colleen on the dock, and together they muscle the fish box onto dry land. Vivienne jumps up onto the wharf. One more heave and the fish box is lying in the bed of the truck. Colleen whacks up the tailgate as Thomas roars up next to them.

"Hello, Skipper!" he shouts at Vivienne.

Colleen strides past him, talking over her shoulder.

"Vivienne's not feeling well. A hard turn in the boat. We're headed back to the lab."

"Seasick? You poor little Townie. You're definitely looking a bit green."

Colleen is standing in the open door of the truck, one foot on the step.

"Vivienne, we have to get moving. I'd like to get these samples processed right away."

Tom turns his back to Colleen and rolls his eyes at Vivienne, hoping for a laugh. Vivienne shakes her head at him.

"You poor thing, you're not looking right at all. I'll swing by later, maybe, give you a run up the lane. When you're all done slicing and dicing." He revs the engine. "Talk to you later." And he is on his way back up the hill. The sun peeking over the horizon.

TRIAGE

THE creature in the fish box is secure in the pan behind them and they sit for a minute in the darkened cab. Not a whole minute, but the space of One Mississippi, Two Mississippi, and Vivienne is glad, for once, that Colleen is tight-lipped.

They had driven down together from St. John's at the beginning of June and by the time they had cleared the Foxtrap Access Road the soundtrack of the ride was mostly silence. Vivienne had chattered as they left the city, filling the small space with words, but Colleen had said: Would she mind? She needed to concentrate on driving. And: She couldn't hear what Vivienne was saying with the windows down. And: Maybe Vivienne could watch for moose? But it was sunny and bright and the middle of the morning, not the dusky edges of the day when moose tended to traipse onto the highway. Vivienne gazed, bored and wordless, out the window at the mooseless moonscape of Butterpot Park. Her ears filled with the sound of wind tearing by.

The only sound now is the sound of seawater against the wharf. The windows are cracked open and a tongue of air licks its way in. Colleen stares at the rearview mirror, hands on the wheel. She snaps the mirror upwards, refracting a ray of early sunshine onto the ceiling of the cab. Vivienne sits on her fingers in the passenger seat, vibrating. The frenzied panic that had threatened to submerge her recedes to a humming apprehension. Colleen turns the key in the ignition. She shifts the truck into gear but presses too hard on the accelerator, spitting gravel, before she recovers her composure and slows to a more Sensible Speed. Still, it is a sickening, lurching pickup ride, Colleen hitting every pothole on the half-kilometre drive from the wharf to the store they are using as a makeshift lab.

The word had tripped Vivienne up at first, *store*. She had stepped out of the truck looking for a converted convenience store—a Susie's Groceteria or a Glenda's Superette. Thomas had laughed and said, "That's a Townie for you." And explained that you bought eggs and beer at the shop and kept your lawn mower and your fishing gear in a store.

The store sits right up against the rocky beach, tucked behind a weathered saltbox in a string of weathered saltboxes. Unlike the well-kept candy-coloured St. John's row houses of the tourism ads on TV, these are dull, their paint peeling. Salt and dry rot have chewed at the clapboard. Fishing nets and crab pots and the posts of long-collapsed flakes rot in the weedy yards. In the long grass hide mangy orange cats.

Colleen reverses into the yard, pulling in as close as she can to the store. She flings open the door of the truck and jumps to the ground, slamming the door behind her. She drops the keys as she strides to the rear of the vehicle but leaves them where they fall on the gravel drive. Vivienne moves more slowly. She feels weak. She feels liquid. She pours herself out of the cab and trickles back to where Colleen is muscling the box onto the lowered tailgate. The veins in Colleen's arms bulge like snakes as she lifts one end of the box. Vivienne traces them with her eyes, traces the way they slither under her skin.

"Don't stand there mooning. Grab the end."

Vivienne grabs. She slides a hand under the handle and on the count of three they lift the box to the ground. Colleen lifts the latch on the storm door and they lift again, two-handed, and lug it over the sill. The fish box is awkward, its weight shifting as the water inside sloshes from one side to the other. Vivienne feels it slipping from her fingers. She grips the box more tightly, digging her nails into the wet, grey plastic, but she trips as she crosses the threshold and her end of the crate crashes to the floor. A splash of red spatters her jeans. Colleen swears and drags the box to the middle of the room. She moves to bolt the door behind her before realizing the only lock is the steel padlock looped on the outside latch of the door. They can lock up behind them when they leave but they cannot lock themselves in. She piles a tangle of nets in front of the door to trip up, to stall, a visitor or an intruder. A cartoon trap.

"We can't leave that in the middle of the floor." Colleen nods at the box with her head. Crosses her arms over her chest. "This place has a revolving door policy." Vivienne is beginning to hyperventilate, her breath coming in shallow inhalations.

"There," says Colleen. She points to the back of the store.

There is a long, dusty, salt-streaked window overlooking the harbour spanning one half of the back wall, and the other half has been sectioned off into stalls. Someone had kept goats in here once, or a cow, the smell of manure rising up when it rains, and the second floor had been a hayloft. They drag the box into the last stall, the one farthest from the door. There are gaps in the floorboards. Through the cracks Vivienne can see the ocean sucking at rocks; the structure has been built on stilts and at high tide the building is in the bay.

They are, all three, finally out of sight. Hidden by a distance of steps, the creature lodged in a place where they will have at least a shout of warning before she is discovered. The women tear apart the hospital-cornered bed. What they can see of the creature's face is grey and unmoving in the bottom of the box.

"What the fuck do we do now?" Colleen thrusts her fingers into her hair and it stands up like so much straw. Scarecrow hair.

"CPR?"

"It has gills, stupid. What are you going to do? Spit mouthfuls of water at the side of its head?"

The gills flutter on the exposed side of her face, like poppies in the wind. The water in the box is bloody. What Vivienne and Colleen can see of her body is this: a finned tail, a sinuous body that barely fits the confines of the box. She has curled her torso like a new fiddlehead, her head at an angle. Appendages that begin with muscular shoulders taper to long fronds, to ribbons draped over the edge of the box like wet leaves. Buried within sleeves of silken kelp are bony flippers. Or hands.

The fluttering of her gills is small. Urgency presses in on the two women. Death is nearby, it is skulking in this room. Vivienne pictures the giant squid forever suspended in its tank of formaldehyde at the natural history museum in St. John's. They do not know how to save her. They do not know where to put her.

Vivienne speaks first. "We are not set up for this. We can't leave her in this box indefinitely."

Colleen says nothing. She stands and looks around the room. Lifts her hands to straighten the collar of her plaid shirt. Her hands at her throat as if straightening a tie.

Vivienne reaches over to lift a length of seaweed sleeve but it's slipperier than she anticipates and it slides through her fingers like water. She takes cooling blue breaths to counteract the throbbing red panic that threatens to submerge her. Her hand prickles where it has touched the creature.

"The freezer. The biggest thing we have is the freezer." Colleen taps her foot as she thinks. "Right. One thing at a time. Round up Thomas. You need to make a trip into Carbonear before the end of the day. I'll make a list. A pump and a long hose. A proper lock for the inside of that door. We'll empty the freezer and drag it back here." Her tapping foot is a rabbit thumping the ground. "Grab a couple buckets and start filling them. We're going to have to turn this thing into a fish tank.

"Christ almighty." She takes a breath and holds it before letting it out again. The rabbit stills. "Let's get the freezer moved first and then you can start schlepping water while I get a few pictures."

Colleen's voice is as white as a blade. It cuts through Vivienne's ears as she speaks. They wrestle the freezer into the back stall and Colleen runs an extension cord. Vivienne digs under the workbench for a pair of buckets and swings open the plank door, kicking aside the pile of netting. She can hear Colleen's smartphone snapping behind her.

Vivienne steps outside into the fresh air. The sky is brightening. She takes a real breath, one that touches the bottom of her lungs. She is relieved that Colleen has acted true to form and taken charge, even if her solution is not ideal. Even if the creature does not quite fit in the freezer fish tank, even though she will have to remain curled up like a snail in a shell. It will do for now.

A skinny bridge runs alongside the building, extending around the corner to the ocean-facing back wall. Only sections of railing remain, and what is still there is rotten and untrustworthy. Vivienne drops off the bridge and onto the shoreline. The rocks are slippery, she is up to her ankles in water. Thomas has told her that the old man who owns the store used to have a wharf that extended out from the deck, used to tie up his dory right here, but now there is only the suggestion of stubby wooden posts crusted over with sharp white barnacles and stringy with kelp.

From the verandah Vivienne is in sight of the community wharf. Other boats have made their way in with their morning's catch, and Vivienne can see a trio of fishermen gutting codfish. Gulls squawk as the fishermen throw heads and fins, spines and stomachs into the water. The birds chase after the offal, diving into the water to grab what they can.

Vivienne watches a pair of gulls play tug-of-war with a rope of intestine, fighting and screeching, before tearing it apart. Each glugs down their share, swallowing it whole, their feathered heads tilting towards the sky. Thomas roars down the hill on his ATV and pulls back onto the wharf. One of his buddies—Paul or Gerard—tearing along behind him. They park their quads on the concrete apron and set to work untying a white dory, the gunwale painted red. Bigger than the punt Vivienne putts around in.

The sun sparks off the water, catching the tips of waves just beginning to form. Last Christmas she and Eliza had decorated Eliza's entire downtown apartment in white and gold—glass ornaments, strings of gold-coloured plastic beads, little white lights strung from the mantle and the curtain rods and the Christmas tree. On New Year's Eve they had turned the house dark, leaving only the fairy lights plugged in, and had caught the twinkle of bulbs in spitting champagne bubbles as fireworks fizzed and popped outside the frosty windows. The light on the bay reminds Vivienne of this. She wonders what Eliza is doing right now, if she is up out of bed, maybe walking Signal Hill, or headed to the bakery for a cup of coffee and a sweet. She thinks about calling her. There are things they need to talk about. Things she needs to tell her. She wants to tell Eliza about the creature in the fish box.

Thomas shouts at her but she cannot hear what he is saying. He waves his arms in slow circles like someone waving semaphore flags as Allan or Paul or Gerard eases the boat away from the wharf. She waves back, a slow fanning. Watches them make their way out the bay while she negotiates the rocky shoreline. As they clear the point she lays her buckets of salt water on the bridge and pulls herself up behind them, bum first.

By the time Vivienne returns with her first cargo, Colleen has gutted the freezer and it sits, lid gaping, in the back stall. Vivienne fills it, two bucketfuls at a time. Thirty minutes go by. When she is finished she leans against the timber post that frames the wooden stall. Her arms ache. Her hands are red, her pant legs soaked through. The creature's face, submerged in the fish box, is now completely concealed by the bloody water.

"We're going to have to rinse her off," Vivienne says. Colleen looks up from the screen of her phone and nods. They position themselves at each end of the fish box. Colleen supports the creature's tail and Vivienne slides her arms under her thorax. Vivienne realizes she is smaller than she had thought, the fronds deceiving. Smaller than a porpoise, more slender, her body slim and lean. Despite that, the fish is all muscle and heavy.

They lay her carefully on the dusty floor. The fish slick with blood and seawater, the jigger still embedded in the flesh of her cheek. Vivienne rummages through the tools on the workbench for a pair of wire cutters while Colleen pours bucketfuls of water over her body, washing her mostly clean of gore. Blood and seawater soak into the unfinished floor, dripping through the cracks in the floorboards onto the rocks beneath the store.

By the time Vivienne has found what she is looking for, the creature glistens. She is sleek and sinuous and green, her tail the mossy colour of kelp. In the hazy light from the dusty window her scales shimmer from green to a swampy gold.

Her gills move intermittently. Her eyes are dull, open but unseeing. Vivienne snips the barb from the jigger, the wire cutters snapping, and eases it from her cheek. The cut end is jagged and it catches the creature's skin and the delicate muscles of her face as Vivienne pulls. Drops of blood trickle down her cheek like tears. Vivienne taps the flap of ragged skin back into place. The edges do not quite match up.

"Ready?" says Colleen.

"Just a minute."

Vivienne untangles the snarls of fishing line, ripping threads of tissue from the fish's delicate appendages as she does. When she is finished, they lift again, Vivienne at the creature's head and Colleen at her tail, and ease her into the water-filled freezer. There is barely a splash as they lower her in.

The fish sinks to the vinyl-covered bottom of the makeshift tank. The women can hear the ocean hissing, the tide rattling the rocks beneath the floorboards like bones. They watch while the movement of the fish's gills becomes an irregular but certain flutter. Colleen taps her fingers lightly against the rim of the freezer. Vivienne imagines she is keeping time with the gears whirling in her head.

"We'll have to manually refresh the water throughout the day until we can get some kind of irrigation system set up. Maybe just pour bucketfuls of fresh water in every half hour or so? We'll have to do our best to keep oxygen levels up in the water until we can think of something bigger to transfer it into. Until we can make the move to the lab in town."

Vivienne's heart beats once. A single, painful strike of a gong.

"We're moving her to town?"

Colleen looks at Vivienne incredulously.

"Of course we're moving it to the lab in town. Have you ever seen anything like this before? This is not a goldfish we're keeping in a bowl here. Apart from the fact that we haven't got the facilities to house this thing, we need to move it to a secure location." She narrows her eyes at Vivienne. "You understand what's at stake here, don't you. This is a delicate situation. We need to treat this specimen with a certain amount of care."

Vivienne nods.

Colleen does not look convinced. "When you get back from Carbonear I want you to do some Googling. Start by looking for any possible species group this thing can fit into—look at deformities, examples of environmentally induced mutations, things like that. We can do some preliminary work here even before we're able to do any formal testing. I have phone calls to make."

Vivienne has not moved. Colleen registers the look on her face. "Honestly, Vivienne. You are not that stupid. She's a one and only. Do you have any idea what this means?"

"I'm not sure yet."

"Well, I sure hope you figure it out soon." Her tone sarcastic. "Grab a piece of paper. We need to make a list."

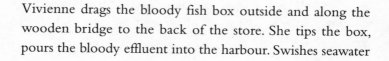

Vivienne drags the bloody fish box outside and along the wooden bridge to the back of the store. She tips the box, pours the bloody effluent into the harbour. Swishes seawater around inside the box and watches as the blood dissipates in the waves. As if it had never been there in the first place. She leaves the box on the back bridge to dry in the sun and heads back into the store.

The wind is whipping up. A gust sneaks through the door as she pushes it closed, sending whorls of dust across the floor, and through the window above Colleen's head, Vivienne can see the waves have become tipped with white. She hears the roar of Thomas's outboard returning to the wharf and a few minutes later the sound of a quad following the main road. Too quick off the dock to have caught anything. The sound of the quad grows closer. It turns in the dirt lane with its row of toothy salt boxes. The women freeze and stare at one another, the creature mute in the corner of the room. Thomas is pulling into the driveway.

Colleen flips open the lid of her laptop. "Go deal with it."

I NEED TO GET HIM
ON THE PHONE

COLLEEN is in the cab of the truck. She is on the phone, talking with Dr. John Isaiah. Isaiah is her supervisor, the lead scientist on the Damson Bay study and is far away, at a conference in Victoria. She has him on speaker, and as she talks she thumbs through the pictures she has taken with her phone.

"You need to get out here. You need to be on the soonest available flight."

She changes her mind about the speaker. Shuts it off and presses the phone close up against her ear. The day has grown muggy and the cab is stuffy but the windows of the green truck are rolled up tight. The doors are locked.

"I've never seen anything like it.... I can't send pictures. We can't take a chance.... It's alive. That's the most important qualification right now, we're working to preserve it as a live specimen but no matter what happens in that regard... Exactly...Two of us and the summer student.... No, she's fine.

I don't anticipate a problem there.... There is definitely a paper here. More than a paper. There's *an institution* to be had here. This is going to make us. Wait until you see this thing. It's going to knock your socks off. I think we should start brushing up on our Latin."

The windows have steamed up. Bradley is standing next to the green truck. He pushes his face right up against the driver's side window, his nose touching the glass. Colleen doesn't see him and jumps when he raps his knuckles against the glass, the sound right next to her ear. She clears a small circle from the condensation that has collected, a spyhole the size of a saucer. Just enough to peep through, but not quite big enough to see the whole of Bradley's face, as if he is peering through a wooden carnival cut out of a pirate at a Church garden party, waiting for his picture to be snapped. Bradley taps and twirls his index finger in a slow circle. Colleen rolls down the window just a crack and mouths the words "Work" and "My boss" and "Sorry" before rolling the window closed again. Bradley is left standing in the yard staring at the closed window, the saucer of clear glass steaming up until Colleen once again vanishes.

Bradley walks over to the store, the muggy air pressing in on him. The weather is ready to break, heavy clouds blowing in, threatening rain. He pops his head through the door to ask Vivienne what's up. Vivienne tells him about John Isaiah from Victoria, Head of the Research Team, and the "soonest available flight," but fails to mention the creature stashed in the unlit back corner of the room. Bradley heads back to the café, promising to meet Colleen for a run in the morning if the rain holds off. Colleen talks with John in Victoria while

Vivienne sits at the workbench, processing jellyfish samples and entering data into a spreadsheet while she waits for Thomas. The creature maybe drowning, maybe dying, while she works.

CANARY

"I'LL be back for you after dinner." Thomas had flung this over his shoulder as he roared up the lane on his quad. Vivienne had met him in the yard when he'd made his way over from the wharf earlier in the morning and they'd made plans for a supply run.

Vivienne has worried over leaving for the afternoon the way you might worry a stone in a pocket, turning every concern over and over in her fingers. She is worried Colleen will need her. Worried what might happen while she is gone. Worried about the creature. But Colleen had said best to keep up appearances. They wouldn't get out on the water again today, probably not tomorrow either. There were things they needed in Carbonear and she wanted the place to herself to start a preliminary report, she'd spend most of the afternoon on the phone and it would be best if Vivienne were out of the way. The reasons piling up like a handful of pebbles.

Now, Vivienne sits on a rock set next to the front stoop.

She has found the keys Colleen dropped in the dirt in the rush to bring the creature inside. She dangles them from her fingers as Thomas pulls up.

"Come on we go." She springs up from the rock and regrets it. Her back aches from the morning's exertions. She twists one way and then the other, her hands on her hips.

The day is still warm but the wind has not abated. Little bits of gravel skitter across the laneway, hitting her ankles, as she makes her way towards the truck. Her hair whips across the front of her face and a lock of it sticks, stinging, in the corner of her eye. She pulls on the door handle and the wind catches the door, threatens to fly it off its hinges. She braces her foot against the inside of the frame, uses two hands to pull it shut behind her. She blinks at the lock of hair caught in her eyelash, pulls it free with her pinky finger. Sitting on the rock, waiting for Thomas, she had been sheltered from the wind by the side of the store.

Thomas blows in beside her, slamming the driver's side door shut. The wind rattles the cab as he presses his foot down on the clutch and turns the key in the ignition.

Colleen had been livid when she'd discovered Vivienne couldn't drive a standard. They had pulled into Damson Bay, were unloading boxes of groceries for the staff house up the hill, when they'd discovered the problem. The miscommunication, Vivienne thought.

"What do you mean you don't drive stick?"

Colleen had pivoted on her heel like a javelin thrower and pitched a look of pointed incredulity at Vivienne.

"You told me you could drive. It was in the job description."

"I can drive. Just not a standard."

"You can operate an outboard motor."

"I can."

She had loads of experience in a boat. Summers spent fishing with her Pop out of Quidi Vidi Gut. A summer job at the boathouse at Long Pond renting out kayaks and canoes, taking little jaunts around the pond in the staff boat to check on inexperienced paddlers, making sure they hadn't swamped their vessels, shooing them back to the dock before dark. She'd talked it up in the interview. She had wanted this job. She had felt it necessary to get out of the city once it became a definite thing, a fact, that she and Eliza were through.

"You can operate a fucking outboard motor but you can't drive stick."

The expletive had made Vivienne shrink. She hadn't seen it coming.

"I didn't know I'd have to."

"You don't drive stick."

Thomas was the solution. A kid home for the summer from the Marine Institute, spending time out on the water, with his dad. Colleen hired him out a couple of hours a week to make supply runs to Carbonear with Vivienne, and to do the occasional pickup from the wharf if she was face and eyes into something, or if she and Vivienne were sick of looking at one another. If she was sick of looking at Vivienne. Grumbling about how much it was costing out of their budget.

"Feeling better?"

"What do you mean?"

"Since this morning. You were looking pretty green

when you got out of the boat. Colleen said you were seasick."

This morning seems a thousand years away. Vivienne had forgotten Colleen's little white lie.

"Much better."

"Not like you to be seasick. Such a fine morning, too."

Thomas gears down as the truck reaches the top of the hill. Vivienne turns to look out the window before answering.

"No. I'm feeling better now, whatever it was."

She wonders how things would have been different if it had been Thomas that had pulled onto the wharf this morning instead of Colleen. Or if had been a Saturday instead of a Monday morning, if there had been people on the dock. What would she have said? What would she have done if it had been Thomas that untucked the slicker from the corner of the fish box?

They say nothing as they pull off the access road and onto the main highway, each of them lost in their own thoughts.

The highway is called the High Road in the harbour. It runs along the top of the ridge that looks back over the bay. The wind, stronger at the top of the hill, pushes at the vehicle. Once in a while a gust hits the side of the cab and Thomas wrestles with the steering wheel to centre the tires on their side of the road. It feels as if the wind might catch the base pan and flip them over. The road is quiet. It is past the time when people get in their cars and commute to work in Carbonear, or even St. John's. They pass only the occasional vehicle.

"You haven't got to me, yet."

Thomas's voice snaps Vivienne's attention away from the scene outside the window. She has been watching the wind blow across the surface of a bog hole, sending loppy waves rippling from one side of the swampy pool to the other. It is barrens up here. Berry bushes and heather but little else in the way of vegetation. A thousand ponds and puddles to hook up a trout.

"What do you mean? Haven't got to you with what?"

"Your little survey. You haven't been up to see us yet. Give us a bit of advance warning and I'll make sure Dad combs his hair. Maybe the week? He says he's half-insulted you haven't been up yet but that's not true. More like you're a dollar burning a hole in his pocket. Someone voluntarily sitting down to listen to him talk. He can't wait to spend you."

"This week is looking busy." Vivienne tries to be cagey but suspects Thomas can see her nerves vibrating through her skin. "I'll see what I can do. Colleen is gone mad with processing samples. Her boss is coming in. Tomorrow or the next day, I think."

"That's what's got her all tied up in knots then. Feeling the pressure, is she?"

"Yeah, she's pretty invested."

"What kind of questions are on this survey of yours anyway? I mean it's not like you're folklorists or something, up collecting stories or tunes. I thought everything you were doing was based on *scientific research*. Isn't that why herself is always hurrying you along with processing?"

"Yes. *Scientific Research*," she lowers her voice, imitating Colleen's rich alto, "and *Clean Data Sets* are what she's all about. The surveys are a way to try and get at some anecdotal evidence. Including local knowledge in your research looks good on grant applications."

Vivienne has been spending most afternoons doing Jam Visits. Walking around the community, knocking on doors, asking to be let in. Collecting stories and cups of tea. Asking about trends in catches, and what species fisherman are landing. What they used to land. Asking about changes in the weather and the ice conditions in the spring, and about anything unusual coming up in their nets. She has discovered that stories are hoarded, doled out one at a time, not squandered to one sitting. She suspects the residents of Damson Bay of taking pity on her as she works her way around the community. A lonely girl wandering around town knocking on doors like a peddler. People meet her on the front step, kettle on the boil before she crosses the sill. Little lunches already laid on kitchen tables, plates of bread waiting for the bottles of jam Vivienne brings from the café.

The jam is both offering and currency. The jars are taken in hand, examined. Tama's reputation as jam-maker glows. What's this now? Strawberry and lemon. Damson and wine. Partridgeberry and cloves? These are not traditional recipes, you know, Vivienne is told over and over. You would never put these things together. Bakeapple and champagne. Imagine that. We never used to have any of this fancy stuff. If you had any leftover berries you might boil them up together and call it summerberry or bumbleberry and that was about as fancy as it got. Champagne in her jam. This said with a shake of the head at the foolishness of it. And flowers in her salads, if you can believe that. What a thing!

The commentary on the jam inevitably turns to a

Harding, Paula
613-243-6502   Feb 18
called

- - - - - - - -
Quinte West Public Library
Date Due Slip
- - - - - - - -

User ID: 22000000740138

Title: ILLO- Luminous Sea, The

Item ID: 32000003029925
Checkout Date: 14 February
2020 16:21
Due Date: 13 March 2020 23:
59

Total checkouts for session:1

Total checkouts.

- - - - - - - -
Thank-you for using
Quinte West Public Library
Trenton Branch
- - - - - - - -

www.library.quintewest.ca
613-394-3381 ext 3322

discussion of *things Tama is willing to buy off the wharf.* Any old ugly fish, she'll take. She'll stew up any old ugly fish and bottle it and sell it off the shelves to tourists who come for lunch at the café or sell it at a table at the market in Brigus to the crowd from St. John's. And speaking of old fish. Slyly. Tama went away, did you know that? With that Bradley. Years ago, now. And can you believe it, she came back with him, too. She worked in restaurants in St. John's and Lisbon and up in Copenhagen from what they'd heard, and how he'd managed to stay stuck to her they'd never know. A swallow of tea and then, he goes running with that other girl down at the lab, doesn't he? Vivienne avoids answering the question they're not quite asking.

She has come to understand that these meetings are about more than the exchange of preserves for old stories, that she has a far more valuable unit of currency on offer. The cove does lively trade in news and Vivienne makes sure when she knocks that she always has a little bit of business in her back pocket. She's seen Mrs. Parsons' new curtains, hasn't she? Are they ugly? Did she notice if there was a rum bottle on Joe White's counter? Just one? More than one? Either one with anything left in it? Is it true that Mrs. Snow has her Christmas tree up out of the basement already? She is taking this Christmas in July business much too seriously.

Once they settled the business of the day, however, her hosts drifted away into the past, stories laid out like the bread and butter on the table. They told Vivienne about the picnics they'd bring up on the barrens and about swimming in the ponds on hot days. They told her about the TB boat steaming into the harbour, and men walking home over the ice from the mines on Bell Island, and about the rows of flakes that once covered the town like carpet, and the smell of fish drying in the sun. Long complicated stories of courtships and tragedies and old grudges that were never forgotten. Stories about whales and walruses and schools of dolphins and about the first time the ocean glowed. Tall tales about the strange things that were pulled out of the sea.

Vivienne wants to ask Thomas what he's seen on the ocean. If he has ever hauled a creature with flashing scales out of the depths. She turns her eyes from the reel of bog and barrens streaming by her window.

"What's the strangest thing you've seen out there?"

Thomas glances sideways at Vivienne.

"The strangest thing I've seen out on the water? Like the sea glowing? Or do you mean sea monsters?" He wiggles his fingers without taking his hands from the steering wheel.

"Well have you?" Vivienne tries to keep her voice light. "Seen a sea monster?"

"Calling something a monster makes it seem grotesque. Like it's something terrible."

"Wouldn't it be?"

"What are we talking about here? One of those deep-sea fishes they pull up sometimes on the trawlers? One of those blind fish with lures that light up dangling from their skulls? One of those goblins that guy in Russia is always posting on Instagram?"

"Anything at all, I guess."

"You know, in their world those goblins are perfect. They have created the perfect adaptation for their environment. They may be a beauty down there. In the depths of the ocean."

"But they're not meant to be here. Wouldn't that make them a monster in our world?"

"You're no stranger to the sea. You handle that little punt like you were born to it."

"I guess so. I spent every summer in the boat growing up."

"So all that time on the water and you still see the ocean as a separate world? So separate that whatever comes out of it strange is a monster?"

"Well, what is a monster, anyway? Something you can't identify with no matter how hard you try. Something so far outside your experience." She turns to look out the window again but really she is looking at her own reflection in the glass. "Isn't it all just fish down there? How can you identify with a fish?"

"Or an octopus. Or a clam. Probably you couldn't identity with a clam."

Vivienne breaks eye contact with her mirror self and smiles into her lap before answering. "Yes, how do you iden-tify with a clam? Can you imagine sitting there letting the sea roll over you your whole life. No feet. No locomotion. Your whole fate decided by what washes over you."

"And that's different than us?"

She is not so sure. "Maybe."

Vivienne rolls the window down a crack. A flurry of dirt swirls through the gap between the glass and the doorframe and she blinks her eyes shut to keep out the dust. A chip bag lifts up off the floor and dances like a dervish. The dirt is accompanied by a high-pitched whistle. She cranks the handle to close the window. The chip bag lies down flat.

"It must be so quiet down there," Vivienne says. "The way sound travels through water. Muffled. Up here must seem so loud to them."

"To the clams."

"Yes. To the clams." Another smile. "Can you imagine? How weird everything up here must seem to anything coming to the surface. The light. The wind on them. The noise." Vivienne fingers the lock on the door. It is the old-fashioned kind, a plastic pin you have to push down in order to lock the door. "I bet they feel like they're suffocating when we pull them up."

"You might be reading a little too much into the perceptive powers of shellfish."

They drive on a little in silence, gravel spitting against the windshield.

Thomas clears his throat. "The strangest thing I ever saw out on the water was a canary. A little yellow canary landed right on the prow of the dory. I don't know if she escaped a cage here on the island somewhere, St. John's or someplace, or blew in from wherever it is canaries come from. But she landed there as happy as a lark, right pleased with herself I think, and sang away. Hard to believe that little girl was there. Sitting at the top of the boat singing. Beautiful as anything. You never heard anything like it." A gust of wind hits the truck like a hand slapping it. The cab shudders. "You know that saying, She sang like a canary? Like a mobster? Maybe that means something else, other than just ratting out your boys to the cops, I mean. Maybe it means that letting things out might not be so bad. That there's something beautiful about spilling your guts, about telling the truth. Like maybe there's something really lovely about honesty."

Vivienne looks back at the girl in the window. Traces her ghost face with the tip of her finger.

"Even if it gets you popped by the mob."

"Maybe especially if it gets you popped by the mob."

"Mighty philosophical, mister."

UP BY THE POND

COLLEEN is lathered in sweat, she is all burning, muscular thighs. She can feel her lungs ballooning beneath her rib cage, every inhalation inflating them fully. She imagines she can feel them pressing against her unyielding ribs—pliant tissue on bone. Colleen is an accordion, sucking in air, heaving it out again. She is burning oxygen like kindling. She is a stogged wood stove. She is an overheated kitchen party all to herself.

She wishes her sneakered feet were hooves—tearing at the ground, throwing clods of earth behind her as she runs. She contents herself with bolting the last hundred feet to the front step, reaching the verandah first, thundering up the dry wooden stairs. The sound of her feet like fists beating on an empty oil drum. Bradley reaches to grab her round the waist in a last ditch effort to win but catches only a fingerful of fabric. He loses his balance and catches himself on the loose railing as Colleen slams her way up the steps taking a slow victory lap around the rotten front porch, arms raised like a prize-winning boxer. Bradley rights himself and bounds up the stairs two at a time. He raises his hand to high-five her, and then curls his fingers through hers.

"You cheated."

"I did not, you liar! Fair and square." Colleen attempts a lighthearted tone but a thread of irritation peeks through at the joking accusation. There is no way he could have beaten her today, she is running on high-octane adrenaline, she is exuding *winner*. The events of the morning, the exhilaration of the discovery, the very existence of the creature, have propelled her along the trail, are driving her forward.

Bradley laughs at her vexation and presses against her. "I'm only tormenting." He lays his hand on Colleen's collarbone. "You're some hot. I can almost see the heat coming off of you. Come in we gets out of the sun." He feels along the top of the lintel for the key and unlocks the door of the cabin.

She would have won anyway, even without the excitement of the discovery like wind at her back. Colleen had run track as an undergrad. Or for the first couple years of her undergrad, anyway. After that there hadn't been time for anything more than pounding the morning-quiet streets outside her apartment building. The asphalt intractable beneath her soles. The hours she might have spent in conditioning or running drills she spent, instead, in the lab. Chasing fellowships and TA positions, holed up in the library all winter and into the spring when the sun warmed the track pitch until the air smelled of thawing soil.

Colleen belonged to the era of VHS tapes and microfiche. She had spent a tedious summer—one in a line of tedious summers—studying video tape of animals running. Comparing the physics of a moose in motion to that of a caribou. Measuring the range of motion of animals navigating bog holes and scrubby tuckamore, seemingly unrelated to their daintier deer and gazelle cousins. Along the way she had discovered an animation composed of a series of photographs of a racehorse on a track and had spent a full afternoon watching it in the gloomy basement of the library. Adding the time to her pay sheet. The photographs themselves she found in a book on the third floor. She had lingered over a single frame that showed the horse with all four legs tucked under its body seemingly airborne above the ground. Proof, the caption read, of "unsupported transit." She had photocopied the picture of the floating horse and pinned it to the wall of her bedroom.

She had specialized in the two-hundred meter. A niche race that favoured neither the explosiveness of the sprinter nor the endurance of the long-distance runner. Not everyone could succeed at the two hundred. Even if you are fast. Not everyone possessed the clarity to see the moment—the instant—when it becomes imperative to switch gears and pivot away from pacing and energy conservation and drain every reserve in order to power across the finish line. She would have made the nationals.

Colleen had found it impossible to settle down to work once Vivienne and Thomas headed off to Carbonear in the truck, found it impossible, even, to sit still. She had paced from one end of the store to the other, peering into the deep freeze at every turn. Finally, she had put on her running gear, determined to take the edge off the manic energy flowing through her. A run would clear her mind. She refuses to let her focus waver, not when she is so close to breaking through, when the ribbon is in sight. She had jogged out the lane and headed over to the café to find Bradley.

The affair has nothing to do with romance or love, though Colleen thinks inevitability might have played a part. Since coming to the cove she has laced up her sneakers every morning, loping off along the roads, leggy as a horse in the misty dawn. The community is surprisingly active at this hour of the day: fishermen already on their way out the bay, lights on in kitchen windows, and in the café. Twice she'd passed Bradley on her way out the gravel road and he'd thrown her a wide-mouthed grin. The third morning he fell into step beside her. They are the only two runners in the cove.

He didn't say much the first few times they ran together, just tried to keep up, Colleen maintaining a good clip and determined not to be the first to stop for a water break. That first morning they ran until they'd made their way back to the café and he'd tipped his head to her and went inside. After that he was there every morning, stretching out his hamstrings while he waited for her. She changed her route so she could collect him at the beginning of her run.

They talked about protein packs and hydration systems. Nutrition and sneakers. Never about the café or when Colleen might be heading back to St. John's. Tama's name was never mentioned. He asked after the green truck—amazed, he said, it was still running—wondered if he might stop by the store and have a closer look at her some afternoon. He'd popped over on a Monday and they'd left the door wide open while they visited. He made it a habit after that to stop in once or twice a week with a tray of take-out cups from the restaurant for her and Vivienne.

The runs have stretched longer and longer. They talk now about half-marathons, about marathons. Bradley has Googled how to qualify for the New York and the Boston. They have started to follow the old shore road, turning away from the coast to make a long, looping circuit through the back country. They run past the remnants of disappeared houses, foundations jutting from the ground like jawbones with no teeth, past berry grounds and trout ponds. Fishing shacks dot the shores of the ponds, little one-room destinations you might end up at if you are out in the country on the ski-doo, or after a few rabbits, or want to get drunk without your wife seeing. Tama's father had kept one when he was alive. It is panelled in tobacco-coloured wood and tucked into a copse of spruce. It is the door of this shack that Bradley unlocks, pulling Colleen over the threshold and onto the mildewy bed.

The air inside the room is cool against their sweaty skin. Colleen wants to be quick, she has figured their minutes in the cabin into her target time for this morning's run, so they keep most of their clothes on. Bradley still wears his T-shirt and his socks and his sneakers, his running shorts puddled around his ankles. Colleen keeps on her sports bra and her dry-wick running shirt, and nothing bounces despite Bradley's energetic efforts.

The bedding stretched over the aluminum cot smells of dust and mould. The first time they ended up here, Bradley had flung back the covers hoping to lure Colleen into the bed, into an afternoon of lying in bed, but the sheets were so threadbare the mattress could be seen through them and they were dotted with mouse shit. Bradley tipped the mattress on its side and swiped the droppings onto the floor but after that they always lay on top of the lumpy comforter, pulling a patchwork quilt over their bodies if they felt cold.

Bradley pounds away with enthusiasm, Colleen's legs hitched over his shoulders. It is this eager-beaver attitude that Colleen most appreciates in him. He is determined to get the job done. The sex is better than average. When they finish, Bradley reaches for a dwindling roll of paper towels and hands one to Colleen. She cleans up and dresses briskly, retying the laces of her sneakers as Bradley pulls up his shorts. She stands up straight, her mind already back at the store. He leans down, taking her face between his hands. She allows him to kiss her before stepping out of reach.

"I can't stay," she says. "I'm up to my eyes in work."

She is galloping across the countryside before he has the door locked. Gobbling up the ground with her feet.

OUT OF THE RAIN

T HE next morning, the rain falls in sheets. It pours from the sky in deluges, the wind lifting it before it lands, flinging it against the window of the café. There is a bear rumble of thunder.

Vivienne and Colleen blow into the café, bell jangling. The rain chases them, slamming against the door as they enter, seconds too late to completely soak them. Colleen and Vivienne stand on the rubber mat, dripping. The mat is made of industrial pile carpeting and it squelches as they step across it. The café is quiet despite the fact that it is getting on to dinnertime. There is only one table of customers, a couple wearing significant hiking boots sitting next to the window, Gore-Tex slickers draped over the backs of their chairs. Otherwise, only the buzz of the fluorescent lights, a tinny radio occasionally jumping with static, sizzling sounds coming through the open door of the kitchen.

The women blink like rabbits, their eyes adjusting to the

light. They remove their coats and hang them on the rack by the door—an absurd coat rack made of duck heads, rainy weather puddle-ducks completely at odds with the kind of weather howling outside the building. Colleen shakes out her jacket before hanging it, drops falling like rain on Vivienne, the tile floor, nearby tables.

Tama looks up from the table she is bussing. "Hiya, ladies. Sit where you like. You've got your choice today, that's for sure." Looking at Vivienne as she speaks.

"We'll park ourselves back here."

Colleen leads the way to a table near the coffee station. She has taken to setting up a workstation an arm's-length from the coffee pot, writing reports and helping herself to refills while Tama works tables. Tama pulls two cups from the shelf and fills them with steaming coffee. Lets them know the specials and the soup of the day.

Vivienne pulls her cup close and wraps her hands around it, absorbing its heat.

"Pea soup for me. And a tea biscuit." She is ravenous. Keeping a secret has made her hungry. "And another tea biscuit. Two tea biscuits." She is already imagining them, dripping with butter.

"It's a bacon-and-egg morning for me." Colleen shakes a paper packet and stirs sugar into her coffee. "Easy over. And tell himself not to overcook the eggs. He knows how I like them." She takes out her phone and begins scrolling. Looks at Vivienne. "I need you to take notes."

Tama, dismissed, walks back into the kitchen. The newspaper lies open on the counter.

"Order up," she says. "The two from the lab." She slides

the ticket onto the line.

"Bacon and eggs, again, hey? That one is going to turn into a bacon and eggs." The kitchen door is open and there is a view straight through to the front door. It is an ideal spot for spying on the action in the dining room. "Five minutes?" Bradley is already feeding bread into the toaster. Rashers of bacon sizzling on the grill.

Tama fingers the edge of the paper. It is open to the crossword puzzle, half-done. Letters inked in the squares and inked over again where Bradley has gotten a word wrong.

"Sounds good."

She stands in the doorway of the kitchen and gazes over the heads of the couple sitting in front of the rain-streaked window. It is impossible, on a day like this, to tell sea from sky. They might as well be underwater.

The man in the window raises his hand, and Tama makes her way towards him, pencil in hand. Colleen is immersed in the tiny world of her phone but Vivienne glances up as she passes and offers a quick smile, as if to apologize for Colleen's bad manners. Tama clears plates and takes an order for dessert. Gives directions to the boat museum down the shore. She is cutting two thick slices from the partridgeberry pie in the glass-fronted case when Bradley calls, "Order up!"

"One minute. Just á la mode-ing these plates." A fat drip of vanilla ice cream slides from the scoop onto the counter.

"No worries, my love, I've got it. I've got nothing to the line." Bradley is already taking off his stained apron and hanging it on the hook next to the stove.

Tama brings pie but forgets dessert forks. By the time she settles away the couple at the window and explains just what partridgeberries are—you call them lingonberries on the mainland, ma'am—Bradley has turned a chair around and pulled it up to Vivienne and Colleen's table, straddling it. His arms overhanging the back, loose and relaxed. Tama walks back to retrieve the coffee pot—refills on the house, let me get the pot. Bradley flashes her a toothy smile as she passes.

"These ladies have been up all night long working, can you believe it? We should think about drafting a contract to supply them with twenty-four-hour coffee, whaddya think?"

Tama pauses in mid-step and looks first at Colleen and then at Vivienne. Vivienne doesn't meet her eye.

"Just one of those nights," Colleen cuts in. "And a few more on the horizon."

"Government contract for coffee, Tam. You couldn't do any better."

"How about that," Tama answers. And then, "Speaking of coffee." She tilts her head back toward the window. She looks down at their table as she makes her way towards the front window. Vivienne's notebook is empty of notes and Colleen's phone lies face down on the table.

WAKING UP
FROM DREAMING

VIVIENNE wakes with a start. The freezer gurgles away alongside her. She is lying stretched out on a lawn chair in the dark, enveloped in an oversized sweatshirt, a second sweater covering her legs like a clinging octopus. She lays her hand on the pebbled surface of the freezer. It is cold to the touch. She is shivering, her toes inside her sneakers are icy. The rain has let up and moonlight seeps through the salt-covered windows.

It is Colleen's turn to make the trip to town. They had finished lunch at the café and Colleen had pulled out in the green truck, heading to the lab in St. John's and then on to the airport. Isaiah scheduled to arrive on the late flight. Vivienne has not met him. She asked about him as Colleen checked the oil in the truck.

"Another thing to manage, that's what he is. Just hitting his best before date." She'd slammed the bonnet shut.

Vivienne is sure Colleen plans to grab him in one hand

and put him in her pocket and grab his luggage off the belt with the other hand and speed back to Damson Bay before the sun is up. She is using Colleen's absence to fill herself up with the creature—the way she looks, the way she moves. She is spending the night at the store, listening to the fish swim tight, angry circles around the circumference of the tank. She feels burdened by the creature, as if she owes her something, though she can't ascertain what that something is. At the very least Vivienne wants to be sure she isn't left alone.

Outside the store a bang. The wind is galing and Vivienne thinks something in the yard must have tipped over or blown into the side of the store. In her sleep-addled state she wonders if one of the pyramids of crab pots stacked precariously against sheds all the way up the hill has toppled and rolled into the store. Or maybe it is a giant bird thrown off course, smacking against the door the way a sparrow smacks against a picture window—a creamy ball of feathers and fluff hitting the glass, the jaunty splash of blood. She opens the door, or maybe she dreams she does, and there lying on the ground is the bird—an auk or a pelican or a pterodactyl maybe, lying in a heap on the ground. It staggers to its bony feet, shaking out its feathers before spreading its wings. Vivienne can see the wind is no match for this winged creature as it screeches and launches headlong into the gale, buzzing the open doorway so Vivienne can feel the breath of its wings, a stiff brush of feathers as it swoops upwards, taking a J-shaped flightpath into the sky. An open maw, the caw at her ear. She shuts the door against the predator. All legs and beady, black, bottomless eyes.

The bang repeats itself and it is only as she startles awake that she realizes she has drifted off again; this time it is not the deep, thick flannel of exhaustion she clambers out of, but a light, gauzy sleep that barely covers her. It is louder this time, the bang, thundering, and she is loathe to open the door. She worries the bird has transformed into a flock. And it is not a single blow, this time, but a salvo, one crack after the other. Bang! Bang! Bang! She will not let it in whatever it is.

Then, the metallic click of the latch letting go. The door opens inward and something slinks into the room. Vivienne is frozen, as if the Hag has descended and settled on her chest. The something that opened the door moves toward her slowly, noiselessly, as if on wheels, gliding across the wooden floor. It does not trip or hesitate at the cracks in the floorboards but moves as smoothly as oiled gears. And then it is on top of her, and she can see it is a head, the head of a person, and Vivienne grips the arms of the lawn chair and tries to push herself back through the holes in the nylon mesh but she is, of course, too big to fit through the holes in the woven material, she has not learned to shrink, to make her body disappear if necessary, and the head comes closer and closer and hovers over her and there is a sudden flash of light shining directly into her eyes and she can see nothing but a disc of blinding white. She turns her head quickly, instinctively, her eyes burning. And then it is sweeping upward, the long arc of a flashlight beam, sweeping up and over her head. She blinks her eyes at polka dots swimming before her retinas, like golden roe floating in the current, and there is a person, a man next to her. Above her. Blocking the little bit of light from the open doorway, the golden spots covering him like fur.

The man leans over her. He is almost on top of her. The fur of light has transformed into real fur, his arm on the armrest of the lawn chair is hairy, it is covered with a thick, black pelt. Vivienne lies as still as she can. The chair is in a semi-upright position, like a seat on an aircraft, and she cannot go backward, and to go forward would mean sitting up and straddling the chair with her legs and pushing herself vertical, into the arms of this intruder. She is trapped. Vivienne can feel the heat of the man through his shirt, through her shirt. How easy it would be for him to settle his weight on top of her. He leans over her and the flashlight beam sweeps into the topless freezer that is a tank holding a creature without a name and the only reason Vivienne can think that this hairy man is here, gliding across the floor and making slow arcs with his flashlight, is that he is a burglar. That he is here to burgle the creature. He must have known she was here because he has gone straight for the freezer and its fishy contents and has not stopped to inspect the generator or peruse the workbench loaded with electronics and small power tools that would surely fetch a couple of dollars on the black market or Kijiji. He is leaning over her and she is trapped and so she freezes like a rabbit in the woods.

Inside the freezer, the fish hits the vinyl wall with her muscular tail splashing water onto the man, onto Vivienne. The man is staring at the creature, transfixed. Vivienne thinks it must be impossible that he has overlooked her, lying flat on the lawn chair, but it seems to be he has. She wonders if she still holds the element of surprise. Wonders if she should continue to lie here unnoticed or if she should shove him away—and then what? Scoop the creature from the tank and run from the store with her flung over her shoulder like a slippery sack of flour?

A pop and a flood of light as the overhead bulb in its little birdcage is switched on. The room illuminated. The shirt above her is a worn blue plaid. The man is large. From the other side of the room a voice.

"Almighty god, Vivienne. This door. Is supposed to be locked. From the inside. Thisdoorissupposedtobelocked-fromtheinside. What is the goddamned matter with you?" It is Colleen. She is winding her way towards apoplectic. She is spinning herself into a rage.

The shape, the faded blue shirt that is a large man, pushes himself backwards. He looks down from what seems to be a great height and extends his hand toward Vivienne.

"John Isaiah. Nice to meet you."

EXAMINATION:
PART 1

Vivienne is wearing thick, black rubber gloves that reach to her elbows. She is trying to hold the fish still on the examination table she and Colleen have rigged up on the main floor of the store. They have settled on a heavy padlock attached to the inside of the door with three-inch screws. Colleen had rolled her eyes when she'd seen it at the bottom of Vivienne's shopping bag but it is too late, now, to head back to Carbonear and exchange it for a deadbolt and, besides, they don't have the tools to install one. Vivienne thinks the word *dead* doesn't fit in this room, anyway, it applies to nothing here. Instead, the situation is frizzy with life. It feels as if they are inside a pop can.

A long, stainless steel table is in the middle of the room. Next to it a second table made from a wooden door laid across two wooden sawhorses and covered with sheets of plastic. Instruments and vials, pincers and thermometers and gloves, measuring tapes and suction-cupped monitors are arranged in neat rows on top of it. The doorknob is still attached to the door and makes a small mound underneath the plastic. Vivienne wonders if they have not made some kind of underestimation when considering door security. It seems as if at any minute someone might turn the handle on the supine door, throwing scientific instruments across the room; that someone will walk up through the horizontal doorway, like that party trick where someone climbs an imaginary set of steps in the carpet behind the couch.

They are working in quick spurts, performing a procedure or two in sixty or ninety seconds before lowering the creature back into the deep freeze tank where she can breathe. It is reverse water boarding, and every time they return her to the freezer she flicks her tail and races ever faster, enraged laps around the perimeter. It is the second full day of testing. Vivienne had barely shaken Isaiah's hand, her heart still pumping adrenaline, when Colleen sent her back to the staff house for a nap. Expecting her to be ready for set up right after breakfast.

They have given up on their initial plan to leave the fish in the tank while they take temperature readings or try to suction a heart monitor to her skin. Taking blood samples has proven completely impossible while she is mobile. The fish snaps and snarls every time they get close to her, biting Vivienne on the hand with sharp-pointed teeth. The mark like the petals of a flower stitched in crewel on her skin. Vivienne's hands are streaked with fine cuts and scrapes; the red-on-white pattern of lacerations and bite marks like the redwork embroidery her grandmother used to stitch. The fish is not quite struggling but Vivienne can feel the muscle beneath the scaly skin tense and flex, and she knows if she loosens her hands for even a moment, the fish's tail will flick from side to side like an angry cat's.

Isaiah lays a hand on her flank and inserts a needle into the IV port installed under one of her front flukes and draws the plunger back to extract a syringeful of blood. The fish vibrates in indignation under Vivienne's hand. The blood is red as garnets. He holds it up to the light streaming through the transom above the door and it shines like sun-soaked stained glass. He draws another vial of blood, and another. Colleen labels the vials and inserts them into a slotted tray before laying the whole works into a blue and white cooler, the kind you might use for bringing sandwiches to a picnic or for transporting harvested organs.

The teeth are an obvious sign she is a carnivore. For the past two days Vivienne has brought her back live fish and crabs after the creature had let the first bucketfuls of offal they had thrown in as feed sink to the bottom of the freezer without touching them. The fish waits still as a rock as her prey is dumped into the tank, kelpy arms undulating in the slight current, uncoiling like a whip to catch her dinner between her teeth.

They had forced her mouth wide to look at her teeth, Colleen holding her jaw open while Vivienne lay on top of her to keep her still, settling her body weight onto her, and Isaiah had taken pictures. The fish foaming at the mouth. Vivienne had looked at the pictures on the screen at the back of the digital camera when they were finished, at the rows of hooked teeth like shark's teeth, and vowed to be more careful in the future.

MELISSA BARBEAU

Yesterday, the fish had swum until she'd exhausted herself but when the instruments had been put away for the day, cleaned and sterilized in boiling water and laid under clean tea towels underneath the plastic sheeting, her laps of the freezer slowed until she sometimes sank to the bottom of the tank. The water was becoming murkier, the crabs starting to get a fighting chance. Vivienne perched on the edge of the tank and watched her, careful to keep her hands out of the water—even though she desperately wanted to run her hand along her flank and try to signal to the fish that it would all be okay. As if she knew if it would all be okay. Three days in and scales were coming off in her hand when she touched her, like flakes of opalescent pearls. The fish beginning to look as dull and grey as wet ash.

Then Colleen had barked at her about the evidence they needed to support their discovery, and the scientific process, and the paper they would write and, goddamnit, Viv, would you get something done, and she was back to work at the workbench, entering jellyfish measurements in the computer database and preparing constellations of dinoflagellates on microscope slides, counting the stars in those tiny microcosms. She was forbidden to look at the creature's blood under the microscope. She wondered what galaxy her blood cells might resemble.

Isaiah had been up into the wee hours of the night, making notes and typing on the computer and he is shaky. His hands trembling. From the collection on the table, he selects an instrument that resembles a hole punch. He inserts the tip of the creature's tail and punches down on it. The tail is hard and cartilaginous and it takes several sharp twists before Isaiah is able to remove a tissue sample. The creature bucks against Vivienne's hands.

"Put it back in the tank. We'll process these one at a time." Isaiah is brusque. He manhandles the chamber of the hole punch open and drops the contents into a test tube. Colleen affixes a label before helping Vivienne drop the fish back into the freezer. Water splashes onto the floor. The fish begins her counter-clockwise laps, though her orbit around the perimeter of the holding tank is uneven, as if her gravity is wobbling off centre. Vivienne watches her unsteady circling. When she looks up, Colleen is giving her the stink eye, and frowning.

"One more before lunch. We'll do another tissue sample." Isaiah walks towards the door. "I'm having a cigarette before we do this last one. You coming?" This last directed at Vivienne.

Colleen is holding a steel tray filled with instruments and used gauze pads in Vivienne's direction. Vivienne shakes her head. "I'll get one when we're all the way through."

Isaiah pulls the side of his mouth up in a sardonic grin as he takes in the two women. Vivienne refuses to look Colleen's way. "Later. Later is good."

"Suit yourself," he laughs, cupping his hand to light his cigarette and taking a deep draw before opening the door. Vivienne is amazed at his inability to read his second in command.

"Take these." Colleen thrusts the tray into Vivienne's hands, the instruments clattering, sliding towards her, as she rushes to take them from Colleen. Colleen looks to be wearing a thundercloud for a hat, and Vivienne has no intention of letting it break over something she's done. Colleen sprays the plastic covering with alcohol and scrubs it vigorously with a clean shop rag. Vivienne pours the contents of the tray into a bucket of soapy water and washes them before plunging them into a pot of water set to boil on a propane burner. Colleen has spread a collection of instruments on the plastic sheeting and is arranging them in a neat tableau on the table. Vivienne looks at it and thinks the composition is beautiful, silver instruments and glass vials gleaming. She reaches for the bottle of alcohol and a scalpel intending to follow Colleen's example and take a turn at field sterilization.

"What do you think you're doing?" The storm cloud breaks and a deluge of irritation comes pelting down on Vivienne. She has not brought an umbrella. Vivienne pulls her hand back, unsure what she has done wrong.

"You haven't changed your gloves."

"I…" Vivienne stammers as she peels the black rubber from her wrists.

"I. I. I. What's that supposed to mean? Get your head in this. Not changing gloves." Colleen's mouth is a line of thunder. "What is the matter with you? It's hard enough trying to sterilize in the field." She is hissing. "This discovery is too important to be frigging around." Her eyes are the feeling of lightening before it strikes.

Vivienne backs up and hits her hip against the corner of the steel table but the retreat has been unnecessary. Colleen has turned away and is striding towards the bench, digging for another sheet of sticker labels. Vivienne reaches for her sweater and heads towards the door, cigarettes in hand.

SMOKING

THERE is a lull in the rain. Outside the store the world is dripping. A thin meniscus holding a pool of water on the edge of the roof breaks as Vivienne closes the door. Rain trickles from the eave and slips inside her shirt collar, tracing a wet line along the length of her spine.

She strides around the corner of the store and nearly runs into Isaiah leaning against the clapboard wall, one foot crossed over the other, puffing clouds of blue smoke. Vivienne taps a cigarette out of its package and leans over to let Isaiah light it, holding her hair back off her face with one hand. She crosses her arms and looks out over the water. Gulls bob on the waves.

"Thought you weren't coming out."

"I changed my mind. Thought I'd get a little air."

"Don't let her bother you. She's high strung."

Vivienne doesn't answer, the irritation already passing. Three months with Colleen has taught her that Colleen's bad mood would pass as quickly as a cloud over the sun.

Gulls bob on the tide, their orange feet dangling beneath them. Vivienne imagines the creature gazing skyward from the seabed. In St. John's—the landscape saturated in street lights and stop lights and headlights and neon-lit box stores—it was easy to forget how clear the night sky could be. Miles of moonlight and stars. A sky to hold hands under, to kiss under. She wonders if, on clear nights, the creature can see the moon or if the ceiling of the sea is nothing but a field of blurry blue. Has her fish ever seen starlight? Or the creamy swaths of galaxies?

"Have you ever seen anything like her before? Somewhere else?" She asks Isaiah.

"Like Colleen? They're a dime a dozen at the university. Girls who think someone is out to get them. Thinking they're Rosalind Franklin, all hard done by."

"Not Colleen." The cigarette between her fingers smoulders, forgotten. "Because I haven't seen anything like her."

"Like her?"

"Like the creature."

Isaiah takes a draw and squints up at the rain.

"Well, that's the point of all this. What we're trying to prove. That we haven't seen anything like it before." He is switching into professor mode, lecturing her. "We are trying to determine if the specimen is genetically unique."

With his cigarette he draws circles in the air. Vivienne imagines he must perform the same gesture in class, drawing circles with his hands or a piece of chalk to emphasize a point. His undergrad students must mock him behind his back, imitating his slow drawl and his ever-increasing circles. Circumscribing their notes, their lunch trays. Circling their lukewarm coffee and their case studies.

"And what if she is? Unique."

"She? It. That's the second time. There's a danger in anthropomorphizing." Out with the ten-dollar professor words now.

Vivienne is eager for the lecture to end. She douts her cigarette under her foot. She would rather deal with a seething Colleen. "One more test before lunch?"

Isaiah takes a deep drag and blows smoke out the corner of his mouth.

"Yes, one more and then Colleen and I are taking a working lunch. We'll need you back this evening to do the sample-run in the boat. We want it to appear as if there is no change in what we're doing for the time being."

From the corner of the verandah it is possible to see along the whole length of shoreline that is Damson Bay. Vivienne watches as cars pull into the parking lots of the post office and the café. She can see people's mouths shout greetings to one another as they exit their vehicles, can see them laughing at some joke, but from here they are mute. There is the sound of rain sprinkling the tarpaper roof, and the wooden deck. Farther up the hill the sound of an ATV. Isaiah straightens up off the wall and catches her by the elbow, guiding her towards the front of the store.

"Alright, let's get this done."

EXAMINATION: PART 2

THE edge of the freezer cuts into Vivienne's stomach as she leans into the tank. The creature has grown wary of her black-gloved fingers, like tentacles, invading the blindingly white tank with its smooth sides and its nowhere to hide, and it is becoming increasingly difficult to lay hands on her. She has developed evasive manoeuvres, swimming figure eights and unpredictable curlicues around the inside of the tank at ever-increasing speeds.

Vivienne plunges her arms into the water and it feels as if she has plunged them into a whirlpool, the suction threatening to pull her in. The fish is deeper in the tank than Vivienne had predicted and water gushes into Vivienne's gloves, soaking her sleeves, her shirt front, leaving her fingers as clumsy as balloons. Salt water stings the sensitive skin of her inner arms, the rubber gloves chafing her bare skin.

On the other side of the tank Colleen counts to three and together they lunge and pin the fish to the side closest to them. Vivienne thinks it will not be too long before they will have to get into the tank with her to wrestle her out. She thinks of the flower-shaped scabs healing on her hands, the fine-lined scratches on her arms. She is not looking forward to it.

"Now!" says Colleen and they heave and shuffle the three steps to the examining table, holding the squirming creature to their chests. Isaiah stands to one side as Colleen and Vivienne wrestle the fish onto the table. He is holding a biopsy dart. The dart is a cylindrical metal tube, a barb at one end and an orange cap on the other. He fits the dart into a pistol and walks to the middle of the room.

"Keep it as still as you can. I'm going to shoot from here. I don't want to risk burning the exterior dermis." He braces his legs like an old-fashioned gunslinger, or a man bracing himself against the wind. He takes aim and it flashes through Vivienne's mind that, if asked, she would not have thought of Isaiah as a sharpshooter, or even a reliable shot, and then there is a loud sound that is the sound of a gun firing and there is a pop of gunpowder at the back of her throat and the creature bucks under their hands.

A noise that is almost a squeal floats from the fish's throat, the sound almost too faint to hear. Vivienne bends to place her ear beside the mouthful of barbed teeth. The sound is brief and then gone, replaced by a gurgling deep within her chest that sounds like water over the landwash. It is the sound of the ocean and Vivienne feels a sudden desire to be underwater, to dive into a cool and moving ocean, to be submerged under the waves, the sun shining somewhere overhead. A spasm courses through the fish. Vivienne hears herself whimper. Colleen looks at her sideways and frowns.

"You hurt her!" Vivienne says this louder than she means.

The dart is meant for cetaceans, for whales and dolphins torpedoing alongside a boat in the open ocean. It is meant to draw tissue samples from animals on the move, and the dart is attached to a long length of neoprene cord that is completely superfluous in the small room. The cord is an accessory, it is costume jewellery. Isaiah unclicks it from the end of the dart and begins to coil it into a loop. The dart stands out of the creature's fluke like a birthday candle. The orange cap buried in her flesh as bright as a flame.

The creature has gone still though the flesh beneath her hands quivers. Vivienne thinks she is in shock but her stupor is only temporary. As Isaiah pulls the dart free the creature awakens as if from a dream and flicks her tail and the women lose their hold on her. Vivienne feels her slipping but her hands can find nothing to grip. The creature flings itself onto the wooden floor, a frenzy of spasming muscle, gills opening and closing. The round wound from the dart winks up at her, a pink eye superimposed on her tail. Isaiah shouts, "Pick it up!" He is nearly hysterical. There is no sign of the circuitous, lecturing professor.

The women have been watching the scene transfixed but Isaiah's voice breaks the spell and they scramble towards her. The creature's movements are slowing. The floor is covered in a fine layer of sand and ancient sawdust and it sticks like flour to her wet skin. The dull sheen of her scales made matte. They bend to pick her up.

Someone bangs at the door.

The movement in the room stops.

"Everybody alright in there?" A hand tries the latch,

pushes against the padlocked door. "I heard a shot." Another rattle, another bang. "The door's stuck."

It is Thomas. Colleen reaches over and grips Vivienne's chin, forcing it upwards until she is directly in Vivienne's line of vision.

"Say something to him," she hisses. Her fingers like pliers on her jawbone.

"Thomas?" Vivienne calls out loudly enough for Thomas to hear her through the door.

"You guys okay in there or what? The door's stuck." He rattles the handle.

Vivienne is speaking to Thomas but looking at Colleen. Colleen's eyes red and hateful.

"Hang on a sec. I'll be right there."

The women lift the fish and quick-step their way to the tank, a strange shuffling dance. Swing her into the tank. A fine layer of sawdust floats on the surface of the water. Vivienne moves toward the stack of cardboard boxes they have pushed to one side and starts to slide them in front of the freezer thinking to block it from view.

Isaiah comes unfrozen. "Colleen can do that. Get the door." Barking.

Vivienne turns on her heel while Colleen slides the stack of cardboard to the front of the freezer. Isaiah turns his back to the room and, using his body to shield what he is doing, sets to work extracting the sample from the dart.

"Vivienne." Isaiah does not turn his head to speak to her. "Mind how you open the door. I'd like you to conduct your business with that boy outside."

Vivienne opens the plank door just enough to squeeze through into the yard. Colleen is right behind her, shutting the door so quickly Vivienne's hair is nearly caught, the bolt sliding back into place beside her ear.

Breathing in the misty air of the yard is like inhaling a lungful of sparkling water, cool and crisp and refreshing. The touch of fog on her face reviving. She takes three deep lungfuls before sinking to a squat, her head between her knees and her forearms on her thighs. She is still wearing the black nitrile gloves and her sleeves and shirt front are wet.

"Christ, Viv. Are you alright? What the fuck's going on in there?"

She breathes deeply again, willing her brain to come up with some string of words that will sound convincing, that will ease Thomas's mind, that will lead him away from the well of suspicion. She strips the gloves from her hands.

"Just overcome with the heat in there, that's all. Colleen's worried about the instruments seizing up." This is not true. "She's got the wood stove on bust." There is no smoke coming from the metal chimney. She crosses her fingers and hopes he doesn't notice. She is red-cheeked at the lie.

"I heard a shot." Thomas spends his mornings on the heathery barrens up behind the town coming home with braces of snared rabbits, strings of wild ducks, oily turrs. He knows what a gunshot sounds like.

"It's just one of the instruments we're using. It's attached to a kind of gun and makes a big pop like that."

"An instrument? Sure sounded like a gun."

"Yeah."

"And the door is locked. That's not safe, you know, if there's a fire or something. These old stores are like tinder."

"That's the professor's idea. He's big on security. And safety, I guess. He doesn't want anyone walking in while we're running tests."

"Or shooting off instruments."

"Using those kinds of instruments. Definitely."

"Well, you guys should be thinking about how safe it is to discharge a firearm while locked inside a hundred-year-old wooden structure while you're at it, too."

"Thomas, I'm just trying to catch my breath here. The last thing I need right now is a lecture from Sparky the Fire Dog. I'm just about overcome." This is true. "I think I might vomit." Also true. She swallows hard against a lick of bile at the back of her throat.

"I'm sorry, Viv. I don't mean to be giving you a hard time here." He coopies down next to her. "When you're ready will we pop over as far as the shop for a Gatorade or a bottle of water or something?"

"Yes, you know what? That would be alright." She thinks it is not a bad idea to move Thomas away from the vicinity of the lab. She stands up quickly and is hit with a wave of dizziness. Thomas stands, too, and reaches out to catch her arm as she stumbles.

"We'll take our time, girl. When you're ready."

"I am ready."

"Yeah?"

"Sure thing."

Thomas swings his leg up and over the body of the quad and settles into the seat and Vivienne climbs on behind him. Her wet shirt clasping her torso. The quad growls to life. Thomas opens the choke and lets it roar—once—before lowering the throttle and making a slow turn in the yard of the store. He takes his time on the gravel lane, and the rhythm of the bike is like the gentle vibration of the boat on a still evening. Vivienne wraps her arms around Thomas's waist, one hand holding her opposite wrist, and he touches them with his hand, briefly, as he drives. For one small moment she lays her face on his back, the worn flannel of his woods jacket soft against her cheek.

They pull up in front of May's Groceteria. The shop boasts the painted Pepsi logo and the painted plywood sign she had expected to see when she had first heard tell of the store. Vivienne is off the bike and jingling through the front door before Thomas has a chance to ask her what she'd like.

TESTING
TAMA'S PATIENCE

BRADLEY'S clothes are piled on the bathroom floor, damp with condensation and sweat. The bathroom is steam filled and smells of wet and heat, the mirror fogged over. He must have run the shower boiling hot, his skin red when he stepped out onto the mat. Water drips down the walls, down the door. The last of the heat lingers, but with the door open, the room is quickly growing clammy. A bloom of mould blossoms outward from the corner of the ceiling. Tama considers leaving the clothes where they lie on the tile floor, letting them grow green and fuzzy like some kind of house plant run amok.

Bradley is up and out the door these mornings before sunrise, hurrying to fit in a run before the morning rush at the café. In any other town this might be considered early—4:30 or 5 to be out on the go—but here there are already the sounds of boat motors and gulls, fishermen and birds ready for their day on the water. A day's work done before they wander up to the café for a cup of coffee when it opens at 6.

She thinks about yelling down the stairs, telling him to come back up and pick up his stuff, that he isn't a child, that she isn't his mother. And he would bound up the stairs two at a time if she did, sheepish and chagrined. Give her a slanted smile and duck his head in that way that used to be charming. Tell her he was sorry, he forgot, he just popped downstairs to check the score of the game before they set off for work.

But she has less patience for his charm than for his slovenliness this morning, and so she bends down and picks up the shorts and T-shirt, the socks and the briefs, and carries them to the hamper. When they were first married, Bradley's charm went a long way. He turned it on to make her smile when she was sad, to make her laugh, to make her not angry with him. Eyes peeping over the top of some ridiculous bouquet of flowers when he needed to be forgiven for some small thing. The charm has kept him boyish, kept him up for a joke, kept him winking at girls. Kept him ready for a good time. Next to him she feels she is aging exponentially, lines and wrinkles jack-rabbiting across her face, while he stayed young. She wonders if he has noticed, too.

Now the winks and jokes seemed tired and she wonders why he bothers. You'd think it would be wearing thin on him, trying to charm her, but it isn't. It is still his fallback position. Winking at her and rubbing his hand over her bottom as he passed her in the dining room. Laying aside his dish towel and taking her hand and twirling her around beside the cold stove. Pulling her in for a kiss on her cheek as he finished prepping for the next day. Or on her lips.

She has seen him running with Colleen, spreading his charisma over her like marmalade, thick and sticky. His eyes lighting up whenever he sees her. She hadn't pictured him for the kind of guy who would take an older lover.

Tama waved to them from the deck of the café, sometimes, as they left to run the perimeter of the community, up over the berry hills. Everyone in town watching them pass in front of their windows. Bradley always turned around and waved back but Colleen would not acknowledge her, and if Bradley was too slow off the mark she would leave him behind.

Tama glances at her watch. It is time to turn on the stove, to flick on the lights at the café. She scoops the used towels from the floor, her hip aching as she bends. She opens the overflowing hamper and stuffs them inside.

OPEN A WINDOW

VIVIENNE hitches a ride with Thomas as far as the staff house.

"I'm going to get cleaned up and then I'll be over. Tell your dad to run that comb through his hair."

She had intended to suspend her Jam Visits until the situation with the creature had been resolved, as if the fish was no more than a tricky math problem that might be puzzled out given enough time, x eventually equalling y, but right now any excuse to be away from the store for the afternoon seems like a good one. Thomas pulls the quad onto the road and Vivienne leans over the kitchen sink, pushing aside the lace curtain, to watch him leave. He disappears up the lane and she turns from the window to face the living room.

The carpet is strewn with Isaiah's belongings. A banged up suitcase lies open on the floor, spilling over with clothes. The house has only two bedrooms and it had felt big enough when it was just she and Colleen, but the presence of an extra body has made the space shrink. Isaiah has been sleeping on the couch. He has not bothered to fold his bedding and the imprint of his body still marks the blankets, the pillow retains the shape of his head. A pair of pyjama pants are heaped on the seat of the recliner and the air is saturated with the scent of his cologne, a woodsy aftershave closer to Pine-sol than actual trees. A half-empty coffee mug sits abandoned on the humpty skimmed over with a layer of congealed milk. There is nowhere to sit.

Vivienne closes the door to her bedroom and strips. She is quick to change, pulling a T-shirt and hoodie from a laundry basket of clean clothes, eager to be outside. Despite the dampness of the evening, she cranks open the window in the living room on her way out.

Once she is in the lane she slows her pace, takes her time walking along the road, past the café. Enjoying the fresh air and the feeling of her body in motion. She takes breaths like a deep-sea diver preparing to plunge beneath the surface of the water. Pushes her hood onto her neck and tips back her head. Fog settles on her face. She licks her lips and tastes salt.

Thomas's house is hidden behind a small rise, a tan two-storey with vinyl siding and white vinyl shutters. There is a neat square of mowed lawn in front and a gravel driveway to one side but there are no shrubs or flowers in pots. No marigolds lining the walk. The house is too big, really, for two people. Vivienne knocks on the screen door, the steel door already open behind it. Through the glass she can see into a small porch. Thomas's woods jacket and a pair of worn, blue coveralls hang from hooks on the wall.

Thomas answers the door with a grin. "Come in, come in."

She slips off her sneakers and pads after him. The house smells of tinned soup. Her bare feet are sweaty and make sticky noises as she crosses the floor. Thomas wears socks and doesn't make a sound. It is the first time she has seen him without his shoes on.

In the kitchen there is a round pine table pushed against the wall and matching pine chairs. In the middle of the table is a toaster lying in pieces on a red tea towel. Thomas's father is standing at the counter shaking Oreo cookies from a cellophane package onto a plate. He is wearing sweatpants and a T-shirt and an unzipped camouflage-print hoodie. The cookies tumble out of the package into a higgledy-piggledy pile like a load of wood dumped from the back of a truck waiting to be junked, whole cookies mixed with cookie-halves and crumbs. The kettle is steaming, water from the spout reaching to touch the ceiling.

"I got it." Thomas lifts the kettle from the stove and turns off the element. "Viv, this is my dad, Clem. Dad, this is Vivienne." He pulls the table from the wall and extricates an extra chair.

Clem extends his hand, his fingers fixed like a bird's claw gripping an unseen perch. Vivienne takes just the tips of his fingers in hers, his grip gentle as a chickadee. She releases his hand.

"For you," she says, holding up a bottle of honey bake-apple jelly. He scrutinizes the label and Vivienne lays it on the table. Looking everywhere but at the ossified claw at the end of his arm.

"Don't mind this old thing," he says, his voice light. "Just seizing up a bit, girl. Oil not getting to the joints the way it used to."

Despite the hand, Clem is hardly the frail thing Vivienne had expected. Not well, Mrs. Parsons had said. Got the old arthritis, doesn't he? Not well, said Mrs. Snow. Don't know how he's going to manage the winter with Thomas back at school. In person, Clem is a solid presence, not tall but broad across the shoulders as if he had spent a lifetime pulling train cars along a track. Or pulling fishing nets.

He laughs when she asks. "Did some fishing of course, but made my trade as an electrician. Pulling wires not nets."

They sit at the table, making their tea. Vivienne fishes her teabag out straight away, squeezing it against the side of her cup. The colour infusing the hot water making her queasy. She pours a glug of Carnation into her cup and stirs until the liquid turns a creamy shade of white. Clem is having trouble with the sugar, his spoon trembling, grains of sugar dancing across the hard surface of the table.

Vivienne turns her head, afraid she is staring. "What are you doing with the toaster? Surgery?" The frayed red towel the toaster is sitting on has bunched, one corner dripping over the side of the table. Vivienne squints and the towel is a red puddle, the toaster bleeding out forlornly on the table.

Thomas wraps both hands around his mug. "If the toaster's not working this fella's going to starve to death the winter."

"Wouldn't it be easier to get a new one?"

Thomas shrugs. "Second nature."

"How are you making out with it anyway?" Clem peers at the toaster's guts.

Thomas takes the cord into his hand as if judging its weight. "This looks good. The connections look good. I'm trying to scrape whatever oxidation is on the posts off and then we'll see. Hoping that will do it." He lays the cord back gently on the tea towel. "I didn't think you were going to make it over the week." This directed at Vivienne.

"You were next on the list. I'm working backwards through the alphabet and I've made it as far as Davis." Vivienne leans her face into the steam steaming from the cup. "And I was anxious for a break from the store."

"No doubt."

"How do you know the cord's not broken inside?" Clem is still considering the toaster, arms crossed over his chest. He leans forward and pins the cord with his forearm, inspecting the connections Thomas has judged trustworthy.

"Dad, it's perfect. Look."

"You should replace it. You can't always tell."

Thomas presses his thumb into his left temple. "I'm going to try the posts first. It'll save a trip to Canadian Tire."

Clem straightens, giving the toaster a little shove. The cord falls and swings, the plug smacking into the table leg, Clem's spoon clattering to the kitchen tile. He reaches down to pick it up and knocks the toaster with his shoulder, Thomas lunging to grab it before it topples to the floor. "Christ Almighty, Dad."

"Don't swear in the house."

Vivienne tips herself sideways in her chair to retrieve the spoon Clem is fishing for but can't quite hook. She is blushing in embarrassment. She lines the spoon up carefully next to Clem's mug and scoots to sit fully on her own chair, elbows to herself.

Clem touches the spoon with a crooked finger. "Thank you, my darling." Thomas rearranges the toaster on the tea towel, coiling the cord into a neat snake. Clem leans back in his chair and turns his attention to Vivienne. "And your making you're way around town. How's your questions going, maid? Finding out what you need to?"

Vivienne is surprised by the direct question. People in the cove usually went about their inquiries in a more round-about way.

"It's going alright. I think I might be asking the wrong questions. I mean, changes in weather patterns and ice conditions, declines in different species. A lot of that information you can find in newspaper articles or old records." Clem takes an Oreo from the plate and crunches his way through it. Vivienne lays her elbow on the table and rests her chin on the palm on her hand. Out of the corner of her eye she can see Thomas has twisted a cookie apart and is licking the cream from one half. "Have you noticed anything different out there, anything changing?"

Thomas devours the newly naked chocolate wafer in one bite. "Nothing new. Just the same things that have always been there. In more or less numbers, you know." Clem speaks slowly as if the rigor invading his body is slowing his speech as well. "I was never on the water every day. Like I said, I'm not a fisherman by trade. And I hardly set foot in a boat these days." He is a long time stirring his tea. "Well, it's funny. I mean I've noticed the bump in jellyfish and those glowing tides and all that, but the first thing that comes to mind is the garbage."

"The garbage?"

"Go down and look around the landwash. Or in amongst the rocks over by your store. Plastic bottles and Coke tins. Sobeys bags tangled around hauloffs." He brings his cup to lips, his hands so shaky Vivienne is afraid he will spill the scalding liquid over the front of his shirt. "It's a funny thing to say but the garbage has changed. That's what I've noticed. People always threw things in the water, the end of the pier was the closest thing we had to a garbage dump, but it wasn't permanent. If the whole Bay had picked up and gone, in a couple of decades there would have been hardly a trace of us. Broken bottles transformed into sea glass. Boats rotted into the grass, ropes disintegrated in the water. Even an engine block would have rusted away given enough time. Now you have all this plastic everywhere and it's getting harder and harder to disappear us."

Thomas listens without saying anything. Licks traces of cream from the second half of his Oreo and dips the biscuit into his tea.

"I cut into a codfish down on the wharf one time and found a tangle of rubber bands in its gut. And I know some of the boys have seen everything from bread bag ties to little specks of coloured plastic on the splitting tables. Once we were destined to dissolve, just like everything else. That's the natural way of the world. All that's left of you a name on a headstone, though salt air and erosion will vanish that, too. Now we're leaving behind garbage that's going to outlast our grandchildren. We've finally found the way to immortality, found a way to keep company with everything ancient down there, and it's through trash."

"Everything ancient. Like what?" Vivienne turns to look at him fully.

Thomas answers for him. "Like giant squid and rocks and old skeletons." He brushes cookie crumbs from his fingers. "Not the only philosopher in the family, am I?"

"Aw, I gets carried away." Clem shakes his head at his own musings. He pushes himself back from the table with his bird-claw hand and walks stiff-legged across the kitchen. "Hang on a minute, maid, I grabs something out of the pantry before I forgets. Thomas, I suppose you can keep her entertained for a minute?"

Thomas watches his father shuffle around the corner before speaking. "Some talker, what?"

Clem reappears a minute later with a bottle of moose meat, pink flesh crammed against the glass, a layer of fat sitting on top. "Fair trade for that fancy-pants jam, what do you say?"

ALL IN THE DETAILS

COLLEEN and Isaiah are surrounded by paper. Printouts of data sets and colour graphs and a stack of scientific journals. The remnants of their lunch are mixed in among the mess—crumpled paper bags and wax paper. Isaiah is talking at Colleen and making notes, tearing sheets off a yellow legal pad. His is rambling, his sentences fragmentary and scattered. He finishes with a thought before his idea is complete and these half-resolved ideas litter the store. They have been balled up and tossed to the floor. They are stacked in precariously leaning piles, they are falling to the floor like leaves. Colleen glowers at the disorder. Her computer screen open to colour-blocked tables and spreadsheets, a moleskin notebook open beside her to jot down stray observations. Each page a methodical list and a series of tidy tick marks.

There is a calendar between them, each month featuring a different global destination. August is Holland. Tulips in a field and a windmill like a pinwheel against the sky. Colleen carefully circles dates with her pen as they work. Isaiah circles them over with a black Sharpie leaving messy bull's-eyes, sprinkling the bull's-eyes with dots—like buckshot—as he talks. Thumping the tip of the marker against the page for emphasis.

Colleen picks up the calendar and counts off the months of the following year.

"A month or two from submission to publication. If we have an article ready to go by the end of September it might not see print until later in the fall. We don't want to wait even that long to announce."

Isaiah is doodling on his yellow pad. "A press conference, then? Sooner than later." He has drawn some kind of bird and a geometric design that looks to Colleen like scribbles. His pen pauses on the paper. "I'm going to need a new suit jacket."

Colleen takes a sip of coffee. It is cold. "First we need to set up a meeting with the department head. Make sure they're in the loop. And we need to be ready to steer that conversation. The university will have their own ideas about how they want to handle this and we do not want to be pushed out."

She wants to act quickly. The less time Isaiah has to envision himself the face of the project the better. His reputation at the university is by no means stellar. His work not particularly original, flirting with shoddy. And there is the botched Adriatic Sea project, holes deep enough in his research method to sink a truck. Whisperings of an affair with an Italian girl doing translations for the field team. Aperol spritzes and sex on board the research vessel.

"That's not going to happen. Research doesn't just spontaneously appear." Isaiah's doodles have sprouted a twiggy nest. The bird incubating a trio of lumpy eggs. "They have to credit somebody."

"It needs to be accredited to us. Not the head of the biology department. Not whoever's signing cheques for ocean research these days."

"Do you really think that could happen? That they'll push us out? We've got great optics. *Seasoned Scientist Toiling in Obscurity Makes the Discovery of a Lifetime*. Great narrative arc."

Colleen looks at her computer screen, at her notes, at the cobwebs in the corners of the store. Anywhere to keep Isaiah from seeing her look of skepticism. She does not have the time to waste mending his punctured pride. She attempts to steer the conversation back on track.

"A quick press conference would be best. We can get the university on board for that. Play the leak line. Emphasize that if we're caught dicking around and word gets out then we're going to be scooped. First past the post means grants. Money for further research. Infrastructure." She lets her gaze sweep the interior of the store.

"Listen, Col." Colleen does not like the diminutive but does not correct him. Isaiah's legs have started to twitch. "If we're worried about leaks I think we already have a problem. You're going to have to do something about the girl."

A scowl. Colleen is not used to taking orders from anyone, even Isaiah. She is the one that has been hunched over a microscope in this draughty shack, stuffing fish into freezers, while he has been eating shrimp cocktail and knocking back drinks and pushing himself onto grad students in wetsuits. She has no intentions of being told what to do.

"What do you mean *do something* about her? What is it

you propose we do? There's no one else and no way we'll get a research assistant out here in the next couple of days. They're not exactly hanging from trees. I had a hard enough time getting Vivienne. And I wasn't exactly scraping the barrel when I hired her, but I was definitely down into the sludge at the bottom."

The twitching has accelerated. Isaiah looks as if he might vibrate out of his seat. Colleen thinks she will need to cut his caffeine consumption. Ask Bradley if he can swap out Isaiah's coffee for decaf.

"She's a liability. If she's going to go all PETA on us, she's a liability. There are all kinds of post-docs who would kill for a chance to get in on this discovery on the ground floor."

Colleen can picture them. All beards they don't know how to groom and hiking boots in the lab as if they are walking through hostile terrain—prepared for sinkholes to open up in the Formica flooring or rattlesnakes. All of them carrying silver travel mugs she imagines have never seen the inside of a dishwasher.

"I think you're reading too much into that little outburst this morning. Vivienne is young. She's full of all that pie-in-the-sky idealism but she is nothing to worry about." Colleen is not interested in inviting anyone else to this party. "You're inventing a problem that isn't there."

Isaiah leans back in his chair, balances it on its back legs. Colleen waits for him to tip over. He massages his scalp as he looks at the ceiling, the picture of someone somewhere else. When he removes his hands his hair sticks up like the twiggy nest in his picture.

"I'll have a word with her just the same."

"Suit yourself."

Isaiah thumps the chair back onto all four legs. "Okay. You're right. We need to be ready when this hits. We need to have the facilities ready to go in St. John's and we need to arrange transport. If we wait any longer we'll be discussing dissection and mounting rather than live-tank options. Though, if it comes to that I want to explore plasticizing rather than articulating the skeleton."

Colleen flips the page on the moleskin notebook and begins filling a clean sheet with notes.

Isaiah rambles on, speaking every thought that comes into his head. "I want as much hard data as we can gather: sea conditions, algae counts, weather patterns, temps, ocean currents. I would love to link this thing to the presence of phytoplankton. Very flashy."

His finger taps a galloping staccato rhythm on the table. He leans forward, elbows on knees, his face close enough to Colleen's that she can see his left eye beginning to jump. She is actively looking for his coffee cup now. If necessary she will swipe it to the floor.

"Maybe we can get you set up with a remote ROV out here."

Colleen looks up. "Out here? I'll be best utilized at the lab in St. John's." She has been expecting this line of thought.

"I need you to collect supplemental data, make sure everything is taken care of on this end. We'll put together a team for St. John's."

"I don't think that's going to work. Collaboration is going to be beyond difficult from out here. The Internet connection stinks. And I certainly don't want to be sending data and drafts back and forth to town by bay taxi."

"Don't worry. We'll pull you out before it's too far into fall. And we can get you into town once a week or so with the data. Give you a break from the boondocks. And you won't have to worry about drafts. I'll take care of that on my end. Start thinking on what we're going to name this thing."

"Isaiah." Colleen's body still while her supervisor squirms in his seat. "Isaiah, I am getting more than a co-author on this article, right? I'm going to be part of this. We're releasing this find together. As a team."

"A team." Isaiah blinks, surprised. Colleen can see his mind whirling, as surely as if the front of his skull had swung open like a door and revealed the clockwork of his brain. "Of course you'll be a part of the process. I mean, we are a team. But, Col, I think we need to consider the optics. Moving forward it will be better to have a single name attached to the find. 'Team of researchers from Blank University?' Too forgettable."

He is saved from further scrambled explanation by a bang against the back deck. Isaiah jumps to standing. His chair clatters to the floor. He takes a step backwards as Colleen leans against the workbench to push aside the tea towel curtains, so thin they are nearly sheer. She peers through the window. Nothing to see but the grey foggy night.

"Probably just that Jesus cat again."

She slides the tea towels back along the length of clothes-line wire that serves for a curtain rod and does her best to cover the window.

"I'm just going to have a look." Isaiah heads towards the door, leaving the chair where it has fallen. He is as transparent as the curtains, an emergent lunacy leaking out of him like light through the holes in the threadbare fabric. Colleen follows him as far as the door and lifts the padlock from the hook. Squeezes it together until it snaps into place, locking herself into the store.

She walks to the workbench, rubbing the space between her eyebrows. Caps her pen and flings it onto her notebook. She had hoped for a different outcome to her conversation with Isaiah, but she is not surprised. His emotional state teetering somewhere between the paranoia sitting like a slippery mink on his shoulders, sliding around his collar bone, and a ballooning certainty that he can steer this ship alone. Into the rocks is where he'll head, if he's left to his own devices. One more thing to manage.

The freezer hums in the corner. Colleen approaches it, hands in her pockets. She has seen the marks scoring Vivienne's arms. The girl knows nothing of self-preservation, managing, always, to keep herself and her fingers within biting distance of the specimen.

Inside its snowy cell, the creature is turning its perpetual circuit. Gleaming in the gloom. She wonders if it's beginning to go mad in the confined space. She has heard of lab rats displaying markers for schizophrenia, of parrots plucking obsessively at their feathers until bald spots peek from their plumage, pink skin oozing blood.

Colleen tries to imagine the play of muscles beneath the creature's outer dermis. A colleague she knew from grad school, a woman she'd last seen years ago, is an animal physiologist, spending her days dissecting roadkill wolves and bear somewhere in Montana. Slicing clean lines in carcasses with a scalpel, peeling away skin like banana peels. Her days occupied with the muscle fibres beneath her fingers, the straight lines of them, examining the endlessly fascinating fact of the animal machine.

But the name of the game these days is go big or go home. Or, alternatively, go small or go home. Making a name for yourself meant surveying the cosmos or entering the playground of nuclear science. Cell division. DNA. Comparing nuclei under a microscope. Untangling strands of mitochondria like a ball of yarn the kitten has been into. There is not room on the scientific stage for the medium.

Something hammers against the wall of the shed, the sound originating close to the floor, beneath the curtained window. Three smacks in quick succession, shaking the instruments on the workbench. Colleen shakes her head, wondering what Isaiah has gotten himself into on the back verandah. Assumes the orange cat has gotten the better of him.

The movement of the fish is so sublime it is a mantra, a prayer. To watch her is to count off a string of rosary beads, to take a turn at spinning a prayer wheel. *Motus orationis.* That's what they should call her. *Prayer in motion.* Colleen reaches down to touch the creature as she glides by, risking the injury to her hand.

SPLINTERS
UNDER THE SKIN

VIVIENNE can hear voices behind the locked-from-the-inside plank door. She raises her hand to knock and then lowers it again. Colleen and Isaiah don't know she's here yet and once she's inside who knows when she'll be allowed to leave. Five minutes, she thinks. One cigarette. And then she'll go in. She backs away from the door and creeps around the corner of the store. The night is foggy and warm, the air so laden with water it condenses on her face, her clothes. Moisture gilding her sweatshirt.

She tiptoes, lowering each foot heel to toe, heel to toe, like a teenager sneaking into the house after curfew, or a thief. The wood planks are slippery. Damp locks of hair cling to her cheeks. She rounds the corner, and startles an orange cat. The cat has caught a field mouse. It is still alive, pinned and squirming beneath the cat's paw. The cat arches its back and hisses and Vivienne recoils and loses her balance, thumps into the back wall of the building. The cat hesitates and then bolts with the mouse in its mouth, scurrying to hide in the long grass.

The exchange with the cat has been a commotion, a small happening on the back deck, and the walls of the store are slight. Vivienne stops and listens, ducking below the rotting window sill, wondering if she's been heard. A body moves between the lightbulb hanging from the ceiling and the window, casting a momentary shadow at her feet. Through the thin walls she can hear the low murmur of voices but from where she is crouched beneath the sash she cannot tell if anyone has peered through the window out into the night.

She sits cross-legged on the verandah, her back against the paint-peeled clapboard. The silvered wood of the deck has absorbed the fog and dampens the back of her legs through her jeans. She takes off her sweater and sits on it, trying to keep from becoming completely soaked through. The wood is splintery and soft. She rubs her hands along it gently, mindful of slivers. Beneath the foggy sky the glowing sea is hazy, the soft light of a scarf over a lamp.

"Hey, Viv." It is Isaiah. Vivienne starts. She did not hear him coming. "I just wanted to talk with you a minute."

She turns to look up at him but the short corridor from the yard to the back deck is all blackness, nothing but pitch outlines. A shadow pushes itself off the wall, peels itself off the corner of the building. Isaiah wipes at the deck before sitting down next to her. The ocean throbs with light. Somewhere behind them the forlorn cry of the lighthouse.

"A lot happened today."

Vivienne digs her thumbnail into the soft wood of the deck, pockmarking it with crescents. Isaiah sitting next to her, his elbows on his bent knees. Water laps against the shore.

"You have to understand, Vivienne. This is big. It's going to change everything."

Vivienne shakes her head slowly. Her voice soft. "I understand enough already. I know what a huge discovery this is." She takes a breath. "But that thing in there, that fish, whatever she is, she knows what's going on. She's sentient. She's aware. What are we doing to her? We can't keep doing this to her."

Isaiah reaches out and begins tapping, almost absent-mindedly, on her knee. An agitated Morse code message, as if he might transmit what he is trying to get across, as if he might send his thoughts from his brain to hers, via his fingertip and her patella. Wiry, black hair escaping the cuff of his sleeve.

"I know it seems that way. That it's aware. But, Viv," regretfully, "it's a fish. And our options are limited out here. We are not in…this is field research. We have to make the best of the circumstances. And this is a breakthrough. It's going to change our lives."

The wood under her hand like velvet. She picks at it with her nail and it peels away from the boards in silvery threads. She can feel her throat closing over. The tears in her voice. "She was in pain. She was so clearly in pain."

"Vivienne. You know a fish does not experience pain the same way we do. Its nervous system is not as developed." His hands begin their slow circling. "You are overwhelmed by the situation. Panicky. And you are projecting those emotions onto the fish."

"But there are rules you're supposed to follow. There

are ethics. And there will be people you'll have to answer to."
She moves to stand up, done with the conversation. "I need
to get to work. I'm already late."

"What people?" Isaiah pushes down on her shoulder,
preventing her from standing. His voice has lost its lecturing,
pedantic tone. "Listen to me." He is angry. "There is no one
I need to answer to. For the length of time we are out here, I
am in charge. I make the rules."

Isaiah moves his hand to Vivienne's thigh, the weight of
his arm pinning her to the deck. "Vivienne. I need you to
show me that you understand."

The hand is unexpected. It is heavy, a dead weight. She
feels a little lop of panic.

"We cannot breathe a word of this for now. This has to
stay quiet." Isaiah's voice insistent. He leans over her, hands
gripping both thighs now, his face an inch from hers. The
light of the moon glitters off his eyes like stones. He is
pushing downward, forcing her to remain seated. He cannot
realize what he is doing. His words are heavy, they have
weight, he is manifesting the heaviness of his words through
the weight of his body. His words are solidifying, they are
being forged at the tips of his fingers like cannon balls, as
heavy as lead. Vivienne is being flattened under the weight
of his words and his hands.

"I need you to understand. You cannot say anything
about this. Not to anyone. Not to your family or to your
boyfriend. Not to that kid that's knocking around." His voice
so soft. "Vivienne. Tell me you understand."

"I understand plenty. I understand that what you're doing
in there is not right. You can't do this to her."

She tries to pry his fingers from her thighs but he is holding her so hard she is sure he will leave bruises. She tries to scoot backwards but she is already against the wall. There is nowhere to go. She pushes at his chest. Warm fleece beneath her fingers and beneath the fleece solid muscle. She pushes harder. His hands move to grip the tops of her arms.

And then he is on top of her and her hands are caught between their bodies, fingers splayed, and she is trying to push him away but cannot find leverage, leverage is nowhere to be found, and he is large and she is small and she can feel her heart beating and his heart beating and still she tries to push him away but he is on top of her and the rough boards of the clapboard are at her back, her T-shirt has lifted, and she can feel each vertebra as the boards rub raw the xylophone bones of her spine, scraping away skin. She struggles underneath him but he has pinned her with the weight of his words that have become the weight of his whole body. He reaches to clench both her hands with one of his and the pressure at her wrists forces her fingers to butterfly open. Her head at the level of his shoulder. His fleece sweater is green and it is soft against her cheek. Pine-drenched cologne and sweat.

Isaiah's voice is a whisper above her ear. "I am in charge. I make the rules. Not the university. Not a goddamn ethics committee. Not Colleen. This is going to establish me. Not in some nothing university department, but in the literature. People will know my name. This animal is going to *wear* my name. I've entertained you but it is done."

He is leaning over her. He fills all the space around her. He is everything Vivienne can see and smell and hear.

"You know what I am, don't you? To the scientific

community? To my peers?" He sneers the last word. His mouth is directly in her line of vision. His bottom teeth are narrow and yellow, crowded into his jaw. His breath stale. "Careers are made over drinks, did you know that? Fellowships are decided over wings and a pitcher of crappy beer. And do you want to know something? I am never invited. I am not ever invited."

He lets go of Vivienne's hands and grabs her between her legs, and his hand is as hot and hard as an iron. She jerks backwards but his hand on her shoulder, his hand on her groin, are like vise-grips and she cannot move. There is nowhere to go. She curls her hands into fists and bangs once against the wall. A shovel laid against the side of the store tips and clatters over. The hand at her genitals squeezes, she can feel Isaiah's fingers moving against the seam of her jeans.

"I am going to get what I want." He gives her a not ungentle push backwards and releases her.

Vivienne tries very hard not to see his face as he stands. She looks anywhere but at his face—at the scraggly patch of grass where the cat has fled and at the grain of the wood-planked deck and at her shoelaces and at the rippling waves. She cannot catch her breath. She can feel a splinter embedded deep in her palm. Isaiah offers his hand to help lift her off the ground. She clenches her hands into fists, hugging her arms into her belly.

He shrugs. "Suit yourself."

The light from the window makes a little square at her feet. She can hear Colleen moving around inside the store. Vivienne tries not to look at Isaiah's face, momentarily illuminated. She tries not to see him but she does. She does.

IS IT TOO MUCH TO THINK SHE'D GET IN THE BATH?

WHEN she'd first scored the job, Vivienne had expected she and Colleen would stay in a postcard house: clothesline in the backyard, rail fence, potbelly stove in the kitchen. Instead, they are living in a nearly renovated sixties bungalow. The renovated part is vinyl siding and squeaky laminate floors and a new microwave. A thermostat on the wall to turn on the baseboard heaters. The nearly part is the bathroom. They had done an informal tour of the house when they'd first arrived and when they came to the bathroom they hung on opposite sides of the doorframe and looked in without entering. The bathroom pink as the inside of a seashell.

"At least there's no carpet on the floor," Colleen said, though there was a fuzzy rose-coloured cover on the toilet lid and a fuzzy rose-coloured mat hugging the base of the toilet and a fuzzy rose-coloured topper on the tank. In the corner a plastic doll with a crocheted skirt and a spare toilet paper roll for a crinoline. The room scrubbed clean, at least, though the grout looked tired and a rusty hard water stain oozed from the bathtub faucet to the drain.

Neither of them had filled the tub all summer. It had been in and out of the house and over to the store and a stop at the café and out on the water and into Carbonear for a run and who had time for anything but a quick shower? They were here to work, after all. And what would Colleen have made of Vivienne lounging in the tub while she caught the end of *The National* in the other room? She can imagine her irritation at having to wait to brush her teeth while Vivienne soaked.

Now Vivienne latches the door, a quiet click, with the intention of submerging her body—her arms, her breasts, her feet—in scalding water. She plans to sink until the back of her head touches the enamel, eyes closed, blowing bubbles through her nose. Until the splinter in her palm floats free from her hand. She pushes the button on the doorknob. Shakes her head at the thought that a lock you secure with the push of a finger can keep out anything. She flicks on the light but the fan, as loud as an airplane engine starting, is wired to the same switch and she shuts it again. You wouldn't hear a pack of coyotes coming with a racket like that, and Lord knows, she wants to hear Colleen coming up the driveway.

Thomas claimed coyotes lurked just outside the village proper. There had never been coyotes on the whole island of Newfoundland but in the past few years they had made their way across the iced-over Strait of Belle Isle from Labrador to the island. Or they had floated over on an ice pan. Or they had hidden away in the cuddy of a boat, toothy stowaways.

They'd been spotted on the streets of St. John's, tracking joggers on the walking trails, and in that isolated bit of woods behind the college. They'd been seen here, too, if you believed Thomas. Padding from shadow to shadow and on the berry grounds and behind the dumpster in the post office parking lot. What would a coyote at the door sound like? Would they scratch and snarl or creep up to the door, silent as shadows? Vivienne hopes she is safe, she hopes the flimsy doorknob holds. She should be free from danger—they don't have thumbs, do they? How are they getting in?

She stands for a long time on the fuzzy bath mat, studying the doorknob, not moving. Looks down and realizes she will have to drag the mat out to the washer, it is covered in muddy footprints, she has forgotten to take off her boots. Her eyes wander to the toilet tank and she watches a drop of condensation slide downwards. Watches herself watching the drop until she realizes what she is doing and shakes herself alert.

She assesses the state of the tub. The sliding door in its metal track is cloudy with film. A glob of slimy soap has coalesced in the corner. It is stuck, she knows, to the enamel. She leans over and plugs the drain, turns on the hot water and lets it run. Steam fills the bathroom. There is no bubble bath, no bath bombs, no Epsom salts. The water is hard, it smells of iron, and Vivienne knows that behind the walls it is eating away at the copper pipes.

She peels off her boots, her pants, and socks. Throws her underwear onto the pile of clothes she has heaped in the corner. Manages the old trick of unclasping the hasp on her bra and plucking one end through the left sleeve of her

T-shirt and the other end through the right, taking it off without completely undressing. The hasp scraping against her raw skin. She catches sight of her face in the mirror. She is all eyes. She is a study in contrasts: white face, dark plaits framing her face. White shirt, and the black bruise she'd received lifting the creature in her fish box to the wharf still colouring her cheekbone. She is a black-and-white photograph. A still from a silent moving picture.

Except then colour enters the frame. Flecks of blue paint, the colour of the peeling clapboard on the store, dusts her hair like confetti. Vivienne turns to survey the damage to her back, twisting to look over her shoulder and into the medicine cabinet mirror. The skin covering her spine has been scraped raw. Blood, blossomed like poppies along the length of her spine, has already dried to sepia. Vivienne's neck kinks from looking, her stiff muscles unwilling to accommodate the gentle twist. She tugs at the hem of her shirt to pull it over her head but the blood has dried and the shirt sticks to her flesh and the fabric pulls at her torn skin, so she steps into the bath half-dressed.

The water is too hot to stand in. Vivienne steps back out of the tub, her legs and feet like two red knee socks. She opens the cold water tap. Swirls the water in looping figure-eights to mix it before stepping in again and sinking under the water until only her face remains exposed to the steamy air. Then she sinks beneath the surface, sloshing water over the side, holding her breath until the water stings every part of her equally. Breaks the surface and lies her head back on the cold enamel rim and thinks about the creature in her tank that is a freezer.

HEAD SPACE

T HE next morning dawns bright and windy. Vivienne waits until she hears the click of the front door and two pairs of boots descend the front step and the rumble of the green truck pulling out of the driveway before heading to the kitchen and flicking the switch on the kettle. What she needs, she thinks, as she paces the floor, is to get out of here for a bit. For the morning, even. What she needs is a buffer between herself and this situation. What she needs is to create a little head room, like the space left in the top of a jar of canned preserves.

She had come across Tama in the kitchen of the café early in the afternoon, early in the summer. The front door was locked and Sorry, We're Closed turned regretfully outwards. Vivienne had walked around to the back door, propped open to let the humidity escape the sultry kitchen. It was too early in the season for berries or apples or anything else Vivienne dreamed Tama might can. Still, there she was in the kitchen after the place had closed after lunch. Pink with heat, a pot of water bubbling away on the stove, a pile of chopped rhubarb in front of her. Tins of spices. The kitchen smelling of an Indian bazaar.

Vivienne had walked in without knocking, startling Tama, and Tama had thrown the spoon in her hand at her. She'd hit Vivienne in the chest, rhubarb chutney smearing the front of her T-shirt, splattering on the floor. Tama had been apologetic: she was so sorry, she didn't know what she had been thinking, she couldn't believe she'd done that. For goodness sakes, it wasn't like there were bears in the woods ready to saunter in and swallow her whole, it wasn't like there were gangs of bandits hiding out in the tool sheds, waiting for the opportunity to sneak in and steal her baked goods. And she surely wasn't going to scare anything off flinging a spoon at it, either. They swiped at the mess on the floor, and Tama had insisted on lending her a faded red T-shirt that was soft and worn, taking Vivienne's shirt to run through the washer. No trouble, a load of cup towels and tablecloths to run anyway. The washer chugged away in the corner of the kitchen. The T-shirt smelled of an unfamiliar laundry detergent.

Vivienne had stayed then to help with the canning. It was her afternoon for Jam Visits, but what a thing if she could bring warm chutney. Colleen was nowhere to be found. She'd never notice if Vivienne was late getting back to the store.

Tama explained the head space business after Vivienne had already ladled up three bottles of chutney and screwed on the tops. The hot metal burning her fingers, scalding fruit oozing down the sides before Tama took them from her and loosened the lids. We'll do these ones over, she said. If you don't leave head room, the jam squeezes out from underneath the lid and compromises the seal. Bacteria will get in and contaminate what's inside.

Head room. Head space. She had to get her head in the right space. She had to get her head on just right, like lining up the double-pieced lids on the rims of the jam jars; so that everything inside of her wouldn't spill over and spoil. She had to get away from here for a little while, to create some distance. She would find Thomas. They would take the truck. There was an errand she had to run in Carbonear. They'd just been in but she could make it sound urgent. Make it sound like she'd forgotten something. She wouldn't mention it to Colleen. Better to beg forgiveness than ask permission.

LIBRARY BOOKS

WHAT Vivienne wants to do in Carbonear is visit the local library and pick up the armful of books she has ordered from the Hunter Library in St. John's. The Hunter is all hushed carpet and delightfully intimidating librarians wearing cardigans and pearls and glasses but the Carbonear library is in the municipal building, with the council chambers and the town theatre, and there always seem to be kids with skateboards doing tricks in the parking lot. Children sitting on the carpet reading Dr. Seuss and old men lean an elbow on the desk, tell stories to the bleach-blonde librarian tapping on the books she is signing out with pointy acrylic nails. The library in St. John's is somehow related to those famously quiet libraries that must exist in London and Oxford, but the library in Carbonear is a closer cousin to a country market or an autumn church sale.

The library is on the second floor. Vivienne climbs the steps and her footfalls echo through the gloomy, concrete foyer. Inside the doors of the book room, however, the fluorescent lights shine bright as Sunday. Vivienne claims the stack of books she has ordered, tapping her toe to the rhythm set by the librarian's click-clacking nails. She accepts a plastic shopping bag and stuffs the books inside, lugging them back down the echoing staircase and through the cavernous great room, every sound magnified. Outside the sun is shining.

Thomas had turned into the parking lot and she had jumped out of the truck almost before it had pulled to a stop. She had barely spoken on the ride into Carbonear and then only to tell Thomas she would be a while, an hour for sure. He never said a word about her silence, just told her that plan sounded fine. He had a man he wanted to see about a trailer. He thought he might drop over to Sharon's Takeout for a plate of fish and chips. She could call him if she was ready first, and if not, he'd wait out by the door in the truck.

She is reminded, then, of the way her Pop stayed in the big Crown Victoria outside the door of Dominion, or the mall, while Nan went in and shopped. He never went in the stores himself, just sat patiently with the window rolled down and waited for her to return. Always in a short-sleeve button-up shirt, no matter the weather, and a hat, the radio on. He would jump out the driver's side door as soon as he saw Nan coming, taking the groceries from her and loading them into the trunk. Vivienne can still see the back of his head from the backseat, and the way he sat, one hand tapping the steering wheel, keeping time with the radio. Hardly saying a word to Vivienne but always handing back a sucker or a handful of hard candy, chatting with the taxi drivers stretching their legs on the sidewalk, smoking and biding their time while they waited for a fare.

Thomas is nowhere to be seen. Another thirty minutes, she figures until she sees him. Vivienne lugs the Sobeys bag full of books to Butt's Gas Bar, a two-pump service station across the parking lot, and then hauls them back again, a second plastic bag dangling from her wrist. She sits at a picnic table set on the lawn next to the theatre. On the other side of the grass is a little pond with a boardwalk and a fountain, and the old railway station. The tracks have long ago been taken up, but a train car still sits at the platform freshly painted and new looking, as if at any minute it might chug to life and take you away to who knows where. All of it looking out over the bay and the plain, pedestrian, diamond sparkle of sun on water.

Vivienne removes the contents of the bag from the gas bar: a bottle of Sprite and an Aero bar. She lays out the chocolate so it is perfectly aligned with the parallel lines of the plank-topped picnic table and fishes the biggest book from her bulging shopping bag, sets it on the table.

The book is large, nearly a foot square, and it is old. Old enough to smell of mould and dust. The book had been called up from Basement Reference. Vivienne has never been to the Basement Reference Room at the library—she doesn't know anyone who has. She imagines it deep underground and cold. The librarians needing to do up all the buttons on their cardigans every time they descend. She wonders if Basement Reference is where she might end up if she could take the train without a track parked across the grassy meadow from the picnic table where she is sitting.

The book is a reprint of a Victorian-era field guide to marine life. It is filled with engravings of mussels and sea anemones, whales and their miniature plankton prey. She pages through it slowly, stopping to look at detailed drawings of the skeletal system of a herring and a cutaway of a nautilus shell. She grabs the bottle of Sprite. It hisses as she opens it, a mist of spitting bubbles as she breaks the seal. The author has labelled each illustration with spidery formal type and elegantly erect Roman numerals. The volume begins with plants—seaweeds and kelps—and moves through invertebrates, molluscs, shellfish, bony fish. Sharks and mammals. She takes a long drink as she works her way slowly to the back of the book, all alone at a picnic table in the sun.

The last chapter is titled "As Yet Unverified Fantastical Creatures of the Deep." There are creatures with rows of teeth, and fish with legs, krakens and sea monsters. All with intricately imagined anatomies, exquisitely whimsical sketches of skeletal systems. And finally, finally, a creature that looks her own. Something with a resemblance, if ever so slight, to the fish wasting away in a converted deep freeze in a makeshift lab so many bays away. She leaves the book open to catch the light. The picture is in colour but it is matte. There is no hint of radiance. No gleam of armour or jewels. She thinks she will let the book stand open at this picture for a little while, she will let this imagined creature soak up the sunshine, let the smell of the salt ocean sink into the page. She would like the wisp of wind in the air to bring a little colour to its pale cheeks. She would like to let the sound of waves and seagulls settle over it like dust, a suffusion of sea and sound and sunlight that she might trap between the pages and release to the gloomy dungeon where her creature languishes. She runs her finger along the spine of the book and feels it crack beneath her fingertip. She retrieves two round beach rocks from a flower bed to weigh the book open while she reaches across the table for the bar of chocolate.

The problem is obvious as soon as she opens it. The bar has liquefied in the heat of the sun. Her fingers are right away sticky and sweet and she is quick to stand up from the table and walk to the nearest garbage can to throw away the wrapper. She is licking chocolate from her fingers, checking to see if she has dropped any on the open pages of the book, when she feels a hand on her arm. A scream escapes her and she pushes away at a body that is right next to her, that is nearly on top of her. She pushes and tries to run but the backs of her knees are against the seat of the picnic table and her feet are tripping against its leg, she cannot get free of it, she is nearly falling over in her panic. And then there are two hands on her, they are holding her by the biceps, they are holding her upright, and a voice is saying, "Viv. Vivienne. Are you okay? It's me. It's just me." And it is Thomas, just Thomas, and his hands keeping her from falling. "I didn't mean to frighten you."

Vivienne jerks away from him. Backs up until she can see all of him, top to toe, in one glance. Backs up until he is far enough away that he would have to step and lunge in order to grab her, if he was to grab her.

"Hey," he says. "You alright?"

"You startled me." She can feel her heart beating. She stands her ground, ready to fend off the slightest touch of a finger on her shoulder, the suggestion of a hand on her arm, but Thomas stays where he is, he is still. He turns without saying a word, toward the picnic table. And Vivienne is seized with panic of a different kind.

"What is this we're looking at then? Sea creatures?" He runs his finger down the broken spine of the book. The book lying open obligingly. He lays his finger under the illustration, reads the caption. Traces the outlines of the tail, the flukes, the imagined skeletal system drawn like the intricate root system of some fantastic botanical. She cannot interpret his gesture. She cannot tell if he is trying to send a signal to the picture in the book, or if he is trying to receive a message through his fingertips. If he is expressing lust or love or if he is giving comfort. If he is trying to read the thoughts of the creature in the illustration, if he can sense that she is trying to tell him something. His finger reaches to touch her painted cheek, to touch the place where a fish hook might snag at delicate skin, so easily torn, and Vivienne is roused awake. She has been mesmerized by his finger but now she is awake.

She is at the table in two steps, pushing her beach-rock paperweights aside, snapping the book shut, stuffing it into the bottom of the Sobeys bag. It catches as she shoves it in, one corner poking through the plastic. She picks up her Sprite and heads for the truck.

Vivienne is as silent on the way home as she was on the way to Carbonear. Saying nothing and staring out the window. Thomas clicks on the radio and hums along to the country channel as they cross the windy barrens.

SICKNESS:
PART 1

VIVIENNE scuffs her way down the long hill from the house to the store. The book hidden beneath her bed, wrapped in a soft cotton scarf as carefully as if in a silken shroud. The road is covered in loose rocks and little stones as round as marbles and at the steepest part of the descent she feels her foot slip from under her, feels her body slide, her arms windmilling. She is a cartoon character, her body levitating momentarily off the ground, a comic book cloud puffing out behind her. She imagines the wind catching her two-dimensional self. Imagines it blowing her paper body over the square houses and the patched asphalt roof of the lab, a faded newspaper flyer wafting out over the bay. Until she is just a pinprick on the horizon.

She catches herself before she falls, the rubber sole of her sneaker on the pavement bringing her up solid. Her heart hammers and she stops to catch her breath, to wait out the feeling of vertigo that passes over her like bats leaving a cave, wings fluttering against her heart, her lungs. She is sweating in the hot sun but the perpetual wind blows and soon the sweat has left her feeling clammy as a fish. She rubs her hands over her face. Her eyes are sand filled and scratchy after a poor night's sleep and hours spent driving. From the height of the hill, the lab is small. It is as small as a doll's house.

The worst part is walking across the grassy yard, afraid someone will open the door before she reaches it. The worst part is putting her hand on the latch. Imagining a hand on the opposite side. The worst part is opening the door.

Vivienne stands on the step, her hand hovering over the handle, before swinging the door wide and stepping over the threshold and into the lab. The late afternoon sunlight follows her in, splashing across the dusty floor. Colleen sits at the workbench entering data sets into an Excel spreadsheet. Isaiah hunches over a microscope, peering into the eyepiece. Vivienne's shadow, long and slinky, stretches across the room to touch him. She feels a shudder of revulsion, and moves so it reaches, instead, to stroke the freezer.

She expects him to stand as she enters the room. To turn and face her, arms crossed over his chest. She expects him to set his feet, ready to box her into a corner. To put his dukes up. Instead, Isaiah barely acknowledges her. He turns his head long enough to note her presence before returning to the backlit world on the microscope slide. Vivienne is uncertain how to proceed. She is prepared for a fight. She is prepared to withstand. She is expecting an opponent. A maggot of doubt wriggles its way into her head.

What she is not prepared for, what she should have been prepared for, is Colleen. Colleen is off the chair and in front of

Vivienne in two steps. She is a bull, a rhinoceros, a steaming freight train. Her eyes glow red as coals. She is not yelling but she is talking very loudly. She is clearly enunciating every word. The maggot burrows deep into Vivienne's brain to hide.

"Where have you been?" Colleen's words are the roar of a locomotive coming towards her. "You have been gone all day. I don't know what you think you are doing out here but you are here to work. Work. You are not here to socialize, you are not here to stage some sort of protest. You are not being paid to sulk. You are not being paid to sleep until ten in the morning and then take off for the day."

Sleep had been elusive the night before. The sun peeking through the slatted blinds before she'd finally drifted off. Vivienne had stayed in the tub until the water was nearly cold. The dried blood on her T-shirt had loosened in the water but the shirt clung to her skin as she pulled it over her head. It had been like peeling off an octopus and once she'd finally gotten it off it had gone straight into the garbage tin. She'd climbed into bed and laid there shivering, fingers and toes wrinkled, and hadn't warmed up the whole night. She drifted off at dawn and got a couple of hours of fitful sleep, but in her dreams the coyotes had gotten through the door. Or had they found an open window?

"If we weren't already so far into this thing I would fire you without a second thought and let you walk back to St. John's. Get your ass moving." Colleen turns on her heel and stomps back to the open laptop.

Vivienne stands in the doorway a full three minutes before she moves. No one speaks. The sun is warm on her neck and she tries to remember if she has put on sunscreen.

Colleen and Isaiah appear engrossed. They are models of hard work and dedication, actively ignoring her. Isaiah scrutinizes the galaxy on the microscope slide. Colleen enters numbers into the spreadsheet, her fingers striking the keyboard so hard it sounds as if the machine she is banging away at is an old-fashioned typewriter with sticky keys rather than her sleek laptop. Vivienne steps into the dusty room, turns towards the deep-freeze holding tank in the corner.

"Where do you think you're going?" Colleen speaks without looking up from her data sets.

Vivienne freezes, one hand on her stomach.

"You're heading out in the boat. I want a full set of samples from the test site. Water temps, jelly fish and algae count, species samples."

"I just wanted to see how she was doing."

"*She* is doing just fine. *You* need to get ready to get out in the boat."

"I'm on my way out the door. I'll be thirty seconds."

Colleen slams the laptop shut and swivels around to look at Vivienne, her hands on her thighs as if any minute she might launch herself at her.

"That animal is fine. There is no need for you to concern yourself with her anymore. You have to get to work."

"I would just…I would feel better if I had a quick look at her. I'd like to be able to say she's doing alright."

Colleen's eyes narrow. "What do you mean you need to *say*? Who have you been talking to?" She stands. "Is that why you went to Carbonear?"

"No. Nobody. I've told nobody." Vivienne retreats towards the yard. Both hands on her stomach now.

"That Thomas? Is that who you've been talking to? I've seen the kind of conversations you have with that Thomas. Always with your heads together. What have you told him?"

"Nothing." Vivienne is finding it hard to catch her breath. She thinks she might start to hyperventilate.

Colleen takes a step closer. Vivienne cowers against the swelling wave of Colleen's anger. Outside, a car rumbles past the store, gravel crunching under its tires, a honky-tonk country song floating out the open window. The vehicle and the lane seem very far away.

Vivienne had expected Isaiah to lay siege. To inundate her with words carrying double-edged meanings, with glowering leers. She had expected him to try and worm through her defences, to strike at her vulnerable heart. Now she feels as though she has prepared for the wrong disaster, afraid the fortress she has built around herself will splinter like a breakwater in a winter storm if Colleen whips herself into a full frenzy.

"You are not going anywhere near that thing." Colleen's finger stabbing the air in the direction of the freezer. "You might as well forget she exists." The world spins faster. The sound of the surf is deafening.

"Oh, leave her alone, Colleen," Isaiah's voice conciliatory. "We had a good talk last night. She knows what's what."

And just like that the sea is calm. Colleen stops yelling. The sudden silence is a physical force. It presses on Vivienne's eardrums and her eardrums throb. She is dizzy with the pain of silence. Isaiah's face a study in composure. Solicitous. The maggot resting behind her forehead splits in half, each half regenerating. The maggots multiply like bacteria until they are a writhing mass corroding the certainty in her brain.

Colleen looks from Isaiah to Vivienne. She is studying them the way a scientist studies a specimen, the way they all might study a slide under the microscope. She moves to stand between Vivienne and the creature.

"Out. I need you on the water. A full slate of bio markers."

Vivienne picks up a clipboard. Turns and walks back through the doorway without a word. Her shadow surrenders the square of sunshine. The room brightens.

Colleen shifts to face Isaiah. "I hope you didn't promise her too much to keep her quiet."

SMOKE GETS
IN YOUR EYES

IT is the next afternoon before Vivienne can escape the lab for an hour, before she can escape the long beam of Colleen's eye tracking her every move. She finishes processing the morning's samples and has a quick sandwich at the staff house. The bungalow is suffocating, as if the air is being sucked from the rooms.

The house is halfway up the hill that overlooks the bay. Colleen has claimed the paths on the south side of town. She runs long ellipses past the cabins and trout ponds on the outskirts, catching Bradley in her trajectory like a moon and dragging him along, so Vivienne laces up her sneakers and heads north. She climbs to the highest point of land and turns her back to the sea. She traces the high road with her eyes, until it disappears over the horizon. She wonders if her calls to Eliza are not going through because of bad reception in the cove.

Vivienne follows muddy tracks, hard-beaten by quads,

and rabbit trails that spiderweb the hills. She follows indents in the grass that lead to impassible tangles of raspberry canes and alders and to abandoned houses, their hearths heated only by the sun. Square outlines of stone walls whisper stories of forgotten people into the ears of rabbits and foxes. The stories are like sighs, indistinguishable from the rustle of grass in the wind. There are livestock still, in places, pastured on open meadows: a flock of high-strung sheep and two furry ponies; a smattering of goats, surefooted and bold. She climbs until her hamstrings shriek loud enough that she is forced to sit down and listen to them for a spell. She can feel the minute tearing of muscle fibres, can hear them knitting together again. Her legs have gotten stronger since she arrived in the bay.

She climbs until she reaches the ruined garden of the merchant's house at the top of the ridge. There are voices here, as well, speaking to her from behind the lupines, from the leaves of a cherry tree. Out of the corner of her eye she catches sight of a torso lodged in a tree, legs dangling in the breeze. She tries to blink it away but when she looks again, the legs are still there. An apparition. The spirit of a hanged bonny pirate or the revenant suicide of a disgraced maid. Then Vivienne looks again and realizes the naked thighs and calves end in work socks and sturdy hiking boots.

"Tama! You frightened the life out of me. I thought you were a body."

"I am a body. Come on up, maid."

Vivienne clambers up next to her. Her tree-climbing skills obviously out of practice. The women sit on a branch in the big oak, as thick around as a fence post, and watch the sun sink in the sky. It is nearly time to report for the second shift at the lab, Vivienne is flirting with being late. Still, she lingers. From the branch they can see the endless ocean, framed by trembling leaves. The branches above them dip into their line of vision, the leaves dancing. They rustle like silk scarves. Telling stories like Scheherazade.

Tama pulls out a thermos of lemonade. She unscrews the lid and hands it to Vivienne. There are green leaves floating in the glass carafe.

"What are these?" Vivienne peers into it, one eye closed. Sniffs.

"Basil. It's basil-infused lemonade."

"I've never heard of such a thing. Basil in lemonade." Vivienne looks at Tama with doubt in her eyes.

Tama laughs. "You sound like those ladies you bring jam to. People don't like it if you fool with the classics."

They swing their ghostly legs, looking out to sea.

Tama speaks, picking up the thread of a nonexistent conversation. "You have to admit it's strange, though. Hanging out here all summer, a young thing like you. No one coming up to visit. All alone in this lonely old place."

"It seemed like a good idea at the time." It had seemed a necessary idea once Eliza had locked the door behind her and told her not to come back.

"You sure seem to miss someone. This girl you're always calling."

Vivienne had counted on Eliza missing her. Missing her and begging her to come home. "I left things in a bit of a mess." She picks a leaf. Splits it with her fingernail. "I was jealous, I guess. Eliza has lots of friends, she's finished school, she has a career. She has *direction* in her life. She's *going places*."

Envious because Eliza seemed to be holding the ace of spades while all Vivienne had was a handful of jokers. It was what they always fought about, though Vivienne wasn't sure if either of them realized it at the time. Vivienne blind to her own faults and Eliza refusing to believe in Vivienne's pettiness. Unable to see the jealousy crawling out of Vivienne's ears and her eyes and, especially, her mouth, reaching its tentacles towards her.

That last day, Vivienne had seen her in the window as she walked up the street to Eliza's townhouse on Queen's Road, the curtain pushed to one side.

"I've been calling you," Eliza said, meeting Vivienne at the door. "I've been calling you and calling you." She didn't pull Vivienne into her arms and cover her face with kisses. Didn't tell her she missed her after all day. Vivienne wondered if she missed her yet.

Eliza was dressed in a green velvet dress that clung and gold earrings that were long enough to pool on her collar bone when she tilted her head to one side, like she did when she was listening hard to the radio, both hands on the kitchen counter. She faced the speaker as if the announcer at the CBC was right in front of her. Vivienne not even close to ready for wherever they were supposed to be going. Still in shorts and sneakers and sweaty.

"I ran into Ann. We walked Signal Hill and then stopped for a beer on the way home. No big deal. I can be ready in ten minutes."

"You're not even close to ready. And I'm already late. I'll see you later." And she had pushed her way out the door, Vivienne stumbling backwards into the wall, into the coat hooks, one of them digging into the soft place underneath her shoulder blade. Blades of hurt digging into Vivienne's belly.

When Eliza came home they fought. About the coat hook, and Vivienne's lateness, the lack of consideration, the taking things too seriously.

"And not taking things seriously enough. I need you to start putting some weight on the things I need, on the things I want. You can't keep blowing me off." Eliza huffed as they stood shivering outside the apartment door, Vivienne smoking. The fight winding down. They had worked their way through all the superfluous sentences and accusations until they were finally speaking the ones that mattered. The only things they meant to say. Rolling billows of fog were romping their way along the ground.

The phrase, *blowing me off*, flooded Vivienne with irritation, though later she couldn't say why it bothered her so much. Probably because it was true. She had put her face right up to Eliza's face, and Eliza might have thought Vivienne was leaning over to touch her lips in apology. But Vivienne had blown a lungful of cigarette smoke into her mouth, into her eyes. Eliza had jerked her head back, coughing. Tears leaking from her eyes.

"I'm not blowing you off. You'd know it if I was blowing you off." Vivienne threw her butt into the gutter and stepped into the house, letting the screen door bang behind her.

Eliza blew her top then, screaming at Vivienne that she'd had it. She called a cab and told her to come by for her things in the morning. Told her there'd be a box on the stoop for her to pick up on her way to work.

"And this job came up, and it wasn't what I'd planned to do this summer, that's for sure, but it paid. Somewhere to perch for the summer." She'd already given notice and her flatmates in the shared house on Freshwater Road had found a new tenant right away. Thinking there was no sense paying rent if she was every night at Eliza's anyway. She'd had two weeks to find a new place to live before a pharmacy student from Malaysia moved into her room.

"This job seemed like the best option at the time." Swinging her feet. "I've had a lot of time to think. Time alone is not a bad thing, as it turns out."

Tama hands her the lemonade. Vivienne takes a long drink. "But you've been speaking to her? Has she forgiven you?"

"I wouldn't say that."

"Forgiveness is not such an easy thing."

Vivienne turns to study Tama's profile.

"What are you doing up here, anyway? Hiding out in trees seems like a funny thing to be at."

"People can't hear your thoughts up here."

"Do you have thoughts you don't want people to hear?"

One corner of Tama's mouth hitches upwards.

"Definitely." It is Tama's turn, now, to be quiet. To let silence sit like round stones in the middle of the conversation. "There are thoughts I don't want anyone to hear about things I don't want anyone to notice. Do you know what I mean?"

Vivienne thinks about Colleen and Bradley running in tandem in sight of every window in the cove. She thinks about all those people up early enough to notice them. The fisherman fixing bologna and eggs before leaving the house to pull his lobster pots. The old man letting out the cat. The café owner making coffee. She thinks about the creature and her golden scales and the silvery wood of the deck at the back of the store.

"I might know what you mean. I think I do."

SICKNESS:
PART 2

VIVIENNE is quick enough down the hill to avoid being late, she is on the button on time. Colleen frowns at her watch as Vivienne walks into the store, door swinging wide behind her. She is ready to reprimand her and frowns harder when she realizes Vivienne has squeaked in under the wire. It is Vivienne who gets to be brusque.

"I'm ready to go." She does a quick turn, grabbing supplies and equipment. Slings a bag over each shoulder and props a plastic bin on one hip.

Isaiah looks up from his microscope, "Need some help, hon?" She does not acknowledge him. Jingle jangles out the door like a travelling salesman.

Vivienne feels as though her surface self, the self that goes about the world, is a weatherman sending live reports to her subconscious. She is in the midst of a cold front, an atmospheric low. She is exposed to the elements and is not properly dressed, she has not brought a winter coat or mittens.

She does not know how to handle the polar air mass radiating from Colleen, so much worse than the slurry of sarcasm she normally sends her way, or the unsettled trough that is Isaiah. She is afraid of sudden changes in air pressure. Of the biting cold. Of ice, treacherous and slippery. She thinks she might beat them at their own game and freeze them out but she is afraid she cannot maintain it. She feels so brittle, she thinks a gust of wind might be the end of her.

Vivienne knows the best thing is to find a way out. She had driven to Damson Bay with Colleen but Colleen is going nowhere until she is good and ready. And Vivienne is sure she could not sit cuddled up next to Isaiah for two hours on the ride back to town, swatting away his scrabbling crab fingers. She wonders if Thomas would bring her all the way into St. John's. Or back to Carbonear. In Carbonear she might catch a bus or book a seat on one of the taxis that make the run to St. John's three times a week with passengers and parcels. She could squeeze herself in between someone heading to the Health Sciences Centre for a specialist appointment and a box of lobsters scratching desperately at the cardboard with their claws. Or she could hitch a ride with one of the people in the cove that commute to work every day. She could chip in on gas.

But then what? She has no place to stay. It is still nearly a month until school starts up again. She hasn't made any calls about a place to live in the fall. She will send out a few texts later today. See if anyone has a lead on a shared house or a bedsit. If worse comes to worst she can pitch a tent in Pippy Park until she finds something else. Maybe work a few hours at the boat house on Long Pond. She can't wait to leave but she is counting on the money. How long will it take the department to cut her a cheque if she leaves early?

She comes back in for the fish boxes and pulls them out into the yard backwards, bumping over the sill. She tries not to look at the freezer in the corner while she plots her escape. Colleen comes behind her spinning the keys to the truck on her finger. Watches Vivienne load the pan without offering to help.

"What time do you plan on being back? I need to know in case you disappear and I have to call the coast guard. God knows we wouldn't want you to go missing."

"Should be two hours in and out."

Despite her efforts to conceal her feelings, Vivienne's face is open, her emotions as bright as an aluminum pie plate in the sun. Colleen thinks she has not been getting enough sleep. She notes the paleness of Vivienne's face, even under her summer tan, the circles under her eyes, the jutting chin. The snap of hurt that surrounds her like static electricity.

Colleen nods at Vivienne's time frame and makes an imaginary note on the palm of her hand with her index finger. She climbs into the cab to wait while Vivienne loads the remainder of the equipment. The ride is all silence, though irritation washes from Colleen in mute waves and counter waves of pain and confusion heave from Vivienne. The rollers collide and break between them. Both women ignore them and look straight out through the windshield. By the end of the short drive from the store to the wharf Vivienne is sticky with emotion.

Colleen lets the truck idle while Vivienne unloads the back, banging at the side of the door through her open window. Shouts at Vivienne as she lifts fish boxes and plastic bins from the back of the truck into the boat. "Just unload straight onto the dock. I haven't got all day long to wait around while you pack in one thing at a time."

She pulls away as soon as Vivienne bangs up the tailgate. Rumbles out of sight without looking back. Vivienne is left feeling like a refugee on the dock. All alone, her small stack of parcels piled next to her. She takes her time arranging her gear in the boat and unties the painter from the post. She pulls at the rip cord on the motor until it starts and eases away from the dock.

The evening is calm, the ocean uneventful. The copper sea unspectacular in its beauty. Sun pennies dapple the water and Vivienne feels as if she is sitting in a bowl of shining coins worth so little they have been taken out of circulation. She eases the boat around the point and heads towards the stacks of the sunken ship, just past the lighthouse. As the sun sinks in the sky, the pennies disappear and the water regains its mundane jewel colours—emerald, sapphire, lapis, turquoise, tourmaline. The ocean extends for endless, monotonous, beautiful miles.

Beneath the surface, she knows, all is wearisome routine. Capelin dart in silvery schools, and codfish, their bellies full after months of gluttony, lazily stalk them. Sharks prowl. Mussels and clams make lumpy pearls from sand. Business as usual. Conditions are too bright to see the glowing algae perform their shimmering nighttime trick. They are instead just swarms of microscopic weeds smothering the bay, depositing a mucus-like film on Vivienne's hands as she leans overboard to collect samples. The runway lights of jellyfish are gone, replaced with gelatinous blobs that gunk up fishing gear and clog outboard motors.

Vivienne takes her time with her work, moving from one wrinkle in the coastline to the next. The sun slides down the sky like butter. She samples and catalogues and marks things on a chart and motors along to the next site. Next year, she supposes, there will be divers and underwater ROVs, robotics with cameras. Tonight she can imagine nothing spectacular emerging from these waters—only slimy, cold-blooded monsters. Clouds creep over the horizon like cats on their bellies. She can smell rain on the wind.

She putts into the bay where she hooked the creature. Cuts the motor and lets the punt drift. She looks overboard. In the shadow of the overhanging cliff, the water is opaque, everything she imagines happening below the surface invisible. She lets out her handline and the jigger sinks, the green line spooling out behind it like silk thread. Gives a few half-hearted tugs but the line drifts and she feels it snag on something on the bottom. She walks the length of the boat, easing carefully over fish boxes and seats until she reaches the prow. Feels the barb release. She settles in next to the cuddy and closes her eyes. She imagines this is how a shipwrecked sailor must feel.

Vivienne is overwhelmed by everything that has happened, by fatigue, by the fear and confusion that surrounds her like fog. By the relief of being so blessedly alone in a boat on the water. The setting sun is warm on her eyelids and she slips into sleep. In a little minute she is dreaming a black-and-white dream. She dreams she is adrift on the open sea, sitting cross-legged on a raft lashed together with rope. The raft is poorly made, and Vivienne is afraid the slightest swell will break it to pieces. She is out of sight of land or the ship that might have carried her here. She pulls herself onto all fours to search the horizon from every angle but there is nothing but the endless sea—no birds, no icebergs, no undersea volcano birthing an island. She sits at the navel of the world and at every compass point there is nothing. She hears a sound. It is the wind or the cries of ghostly sailors. She strains her ears to hear.

Below the surface of the water, and just out of reach of the raft, a flash of light. Vivienne crawls until she is at the very edge of her rickety craft and peers into the blackness. There is something there, gleaming like silver. She cannot tell if it is a school of fish—herring or mackerel—or the armour of a long-dead conquistador. The raft is tippy. She uses one hand to grip the rough lumber and reaches with the other to touch whatever it is that lies just out of sight. Her hand is in the salty sea. The skin of the ocean, the first eighth of an inch, has been warmed by the sun, but Vivienne can feel the frigidity of the deep radiating into her palm from some bottomless trench. And then something takes hold of her hand. It is pulling her in.

She wakes with a start, bumping her head against the inside flank of the punt. There is something tugging on the line. She stands up, groggy and unsure of her feet, and pulls the line in, hand over hand. It is heavy and she pulls quickly hoping to use momentum to drag whatever she has caught over the gunwale. Her heart pounds. It has accelerated from a quiet adagio to a rabbity presto in a matter of seconds. She watches a shadow materialize and jumps back as she wrenches her catch into the boat, nearly losing her balance. It is a massive, wriggling sculpin. Warty and ugly, it looks like a wet tumour, and she would not be surprised to see lumpy growths of hair or teeth sprouting from its flesh. It gapes at her with bulging eyes and flaps its fleshy lips at her. Vivienne watches it twitch its way along the bottom of the boat. She pulls the jigger from its lip before catching it by its ravaged tail with the grappling hook and sending it flying back into the sea. She will not keep it as a sample, she does not mark its existence on her sheet. Instead, she starts the motor and heads back to the wharf. The prow of the punt is scummy with algae, the motor churns up jellyfish in its wake.

Colleen is not at the dock when she arrives, so Vivienne ties up the boat by herself and stacks her pile of fish boxes and bins. A boatload of fishermen with their evening's catch wave at her from further down the wharf. They are splitting fish and drinking Blue Star. She waves back but doesn't walk the length of the wharf to speak to them, pretending, instead, to be engrossed in her numbers and charts as she waits for the truck. By the time Colleen pulls up, exhaustion is overtaking her. She spends five plodding minutes loading the back before Colleen jumps down from the cab to help her lift the bigger things into the pan. They drive to the store in silence, though the waves of tension have lessened and there is only a little swell on the water between them.

The store is dark when they arrive.

"Where's Isaiah?" Vivienne has not meant to ask, but the words are out of her mouth before she knows they are there.

"Is it necessary for you to know his comings and goings? Are you organizing his social calendar, now?" But Colleen relents. "Gone up to the house. You're on night watch here for the next couple of days. We're not leaving the sample alone from here on out. Despite the implementation of our advanced security system," she shakes her head at the padlock, "a kid with a bobby pin could break in here if they wanted to."

Vivienne shrugs. A night spent in the store infinitely more appealing than lying in her room with her eyes open and only a blanket to protect her from anyone who might stumble upon her in the dark. She is not worried about the kids with their hairpin lock picks.

Colleen is all details. She is running down her list like a harried mother briefing the babysitter. Blitzing her way through so she can get out the door before someone starts crying. "There's a cot and a sleeping bag in the corner. You've been upgraded from the lawn chair."

"Okay. I'm fine with that."

"Process what you collected tonight before you settle in. I'm considering you on-shift until...," Colleen looks at her watch. "Ten. No company. I don't want to find out that Thomas was here."

Vivienne lays down what she has been carrying and walks towards the freezer in the corner. She has not seen the creature since the morning of the dart gun. Two full days. Colleen has been running interference, keeping Vivienne away from her, and Vivienne knows she is being punished. Still, now that she has been assigned night duty the point seems moot. Colleen steps in front of her before she reaches the tank. She is not quite ready to acquiesce.

"Once you get the samples processed I need you to start entering data into the spreadsheet. It would be a good use of your time if you started working on that tonight as well."

"I can do that." In their tired states, Vivienne and Colleen have settled into old routines, a workable back and forth. Vivienne sees an opportunity yawn open like a cave. She had not thought she could talk to Colleen about what happened on the back deck of the store in the dark. But they are alone and surely she can trust her. "Colleen. Can I talk to you about something?"

"Vivienne. I don't want to hear this again. We are working on getting that animal to St. John's and once we get her there we can set her up in a proper tank. This is temporary."

Vivienne does not know how to block Colleen's flow of words, how to steer the conversation in the direction she wants it to go.

Colleen is still talking. "Monday morning we're going to make arrangements with the lab in town to transport her to St. John's in something that's not a fish box. And not a freezer. And not a laundry basket or whatever else lunatic thing we think we can rig up. I might have to go in and coordinate some things from there. We're starting to run out of time."

"You and Isaiah are both going in?"

"Again with the social secretary business." Colleen cracks her knuckles in irritation but answers Vivienne's question. "I'm going. He'll stay. We'd like one of us here."

"I'd rather come with you, then."

"You'd rather come with me? In the truck? You'd rather come with me in the truck?" Colleen is eyeing her skeptically.

"I'm not comfortable here anymore. By myself."

"Since when? You've been out here all summer. That thing is not going to crawl out of the freezer and eat you."

"I'm not comfortable with him." She takes a breath. Studies the grain of the wood floor. "I don't want to be here with him by myself."

"With who?"

She looks up at the question. "With Isaiah."

"Isaiah? What's that's supposed to mean?" Colleen looks Vivienne in the eye. She does not blink. Vivienne thinks this is the way she must peer into a microscope. She wonders if all the little microorganisms can see this giant eye staring down at them unblinking. She wonders if they all swim to the edges of the slide, trying to escape her glare.

"Things have gone badly with us." These are not quite the right words. She tries again. "He wasn't nice."

"Despite what you might think, he doesn't need to be nice to you."

"No. He doesn't." Even Vivienne can see this is true. "But he wasn't appropriate." She cannot make herself speak what happened. "He tried something. He tried to do something to me."

"He tried to do something to you." Colleen is peering at her. Studying her face the way she might a drop of blood on a microscope slide.

"It happened. I'm not making it up." Vivienne's voice is as small as a penny. Outside the windows a gull cries.

"Vivienne." Colleen is, for once, not yelling. "I'm not saying it didn't happen." She drops her hands. "But it doesn't matter. It doesn't matter that you're not making it up. It's your word and his word." There is no trace of irritation or annoyance in her voice. She is speaking so quietly. "Do you really want to go around telling people this? It will do you no good. It will do the project no good."

The women face each other, a foot apart. Their bodies held in mirror image, their arms hanging by their sides.

"I know you think telling people this will make you feel better. You think there is someone out there that can help you, somehow. But Vivienne. No one is going to stroke your hair and tell you it's going to be alright, that everything will be fine. You think that's what's going to happen. But it won't."

Vivienne is dizzy. She feels a mounting pressure in her head. Her brain feels as if it has expanded and grown too large for her skull. Blood pounds against bone. And she is tired. She needs to lie down. She thinks she will pass out on the floor if she doesn't lie down this instant.

Colleen is still talking. "Telling anyone else about this will not make things better for you. Your story will be like one of those dolphins. Have you seen them? The dolphins?" She is using her most reasonable voice. Vivienne barely recognizes it. "Down in one of the Carolinas. Or Florida, maybe. This dolphin swam right into the beach where all those Spring Breakers were getting pissed, and someone spotted it and hauled it in and everyone had a picture with it, everyone got a selfie, and rubbed their tits on it, and the next thing they knew it was dead. Mauled to death."

Vivienne sweeps her eyes around the room searching for the cot.

"That's what will happen to your story if you put it out there. That's what they'll do to you. There are people out there that will tear it apart. That will tear you apart."

Vivienne wonders if the sleeping bag is the kind you can zip over your head. The kind you can make a cocoon of and disappear into.

"I am not saying this to be mean, Vivienne. I am not trying to be hard." Colleen gives her head a single shake. Like she has just seen something unfortunate. Like a flat tire. Or a rabbit killed on the highway. "I'm just being pragmatic. I'm glad you told me this. I'm glad you got it off your chest. And I will make sure nothing else happens while you're out here. But what good will it be to tell anyone else? People who will say you made it up, especially when news of the specimen gets out. They'll say you're trying to bring attention to yourself. They will call you a slut. They will call it to your face. They will call your house fifty times in a night and tell it to you over the phone. And no matter who you tell you will have to deal with that part by yourself. I am just trying to say: be practical. I am saying: think about what you're doing. Not everyone is a good person, you know."

Colleen reaches to touch Vivienne on the shoulder. Vivienne twitches her arm away and pushes past her to look at the creature in the freezer. The air gushes from her lungs.

As soon as Colleen had mentioned the night watch it had occurred to Vivienne to try and win the creature over. She'd had a flash of hand-feeding her capelin from the tub next to the workbench, murmuring to her through the night. She'd thought to lull her with stories. She wants to tell the fish the colour of the sea today. About the sun pennies on the bay, and she would not make them seem like worthless currency, but treasure just out of reach. She wants to gossip about the jellyfish that are gaining the bay and the gulls and the dogfish that stalks the old sunken ship with its garden of kelp, swaying in the tide like ribbons. Vivienne hopes she might convince her by the tone of her voice and her body language that she is a friend, not an enemy. That she is in her corner for as long as she is out here. She hopes she might convince her sea monster that she will not abandon her.

But what she sees in the tank shocks her out of her daydream. The creature is lying on the bottom of the tank, the water a dingy grey. Her gleaming armour, her scaled metallic chest plate, is dull. Vivienne thinks she is dead. Her own lungs have stopped working. She feels as if she is smothering.

She exhales as the creature twitches and makes one slow rotation of the freezer before sinking to the bottom again. No elegantly livid circles. No thrashing. No fury. The round wound where the dart had pierced her flesh is red and looks infected. The fish kicks up again, with effort, and makes another listless turn. Vivienne trails her hand through the water and this time the fish senses her. She makes a quick, feeble dart at the surface, towards the fingers Vivienne has let drift in the water, but her aim is short, as if her depth perception has been disabled. Her gills flutter irregularly. The wound in her cheek is a throbbing lump the size of a sea urchin. As she turns from Vivienne's hand, she bumps her face off the side of the freezer. The boil pops and stringy green pus explodes from the side of her face. She recoils like a snail into its shell at the touch of a finger. Her excursion to the top of the tank seems to have exhausted her and she once again sinks to the bottom. A skim of grey scales coat the surface of the water.

IN BEHIND THE
WHIPPER SNIPPER

COLLEEN leans against a pressure treated post, the wood smooth beneath her cheek. The chemical smell of the post mingles with odours from inside the café, the sharp tang of vinegar and something herby she can't put her finger on. She is standing beneath the back deck of the coffee shop, out of sight of the kitchen. Through the screen door she can hear Tama's efficient movements as she bustles about: the clatter of dishes, taps turning on and off, the cling clang of metal utensils. The radio is in and out, the sound woolly with static; old-timey country singers more gravelly than they need to be, the sliding notes of steel guitars bending like spoons. And yet Tama keeps the evening show playing. Broadcasting a misplaced optimism that—sooner or later—she will get a clear signal.

Colleen keeps to the shadows, picturing Vivienne's pale moon face as she barred the door. She wonders if she is afraid of the dark. She has let Vivienne believe she left the store to meet directly with Isaiah but she has other business to attend to first. Loose ends to tie. She hears Bradley, his voice boisterous and loud, as he enters the kitchen. The noise Tama makes as she works is part of the natural soundscape of the café, even the squelch of her sneakers, the metallic rasp of whisk on bowl. She is not quiet—Colleen can map her movements by ear, but her auditory presence in the space is part of the ambient noise. Bradley, by contrast, jangles and clangs. He disrupts the beat Tama is keeping, muddles the meter. Colleen can hear him cross the floor—he must be wearing his heavy boots—his footsteps causing a spoon left in a teacup on the patio to ping like a triangle in an orchestra. He pauses to talk to Tama. The conversation is lopsided, booming and murmuring, booming then murmuring, and then he bursts through the doorway in a gush of childish energy. The deck shakes as he pounds down the stairs.

Colleen steps away from the deck post and drifts out into the light. Bradley catches sight of her. Wiggling his eyebrows he spreads his fingers wide, moving towards her as if to grab her by the ribs. She frowns and puts a finger to her lips. Points at a shadowy place at the back of the property. Bradley ignores this direction and pulls her close, plants a kiss on her neck. She pushes him away and creeps towards the back of the yard. She does not turn to see if he is following.

Beyond the back deck is a grassy lawn and a handful of wooden tables with holes at their centre for umbrellas, though it is usually too windy to use them. The chairs are stacked under the deck for the night, looking as if they might tip over at any minute. Beyond the lawn, the garden slopes towards the bay. Tama has planned rows of raised garden boxes but for now the few she has built are empty; there are only a handful of pots planted with herbs, basil and parsley. To the right a pile of topsoil covered with a pelt of weeds and to the left a tiny shed and a hulking plastic compost bin surrounded by a scattering of broken eggshells, a rat trap peeking out behind it.

Colleen sits on a garden box and looks out over the harbour, fiddling with the truck keys still in her hand. The café is set partway up the sloping bowl that makes up Damson Bay. The high road above them, and below the water and the lighthouse and the wharf. In the dark, the town is a broken dish of lights, rimmed at its jagged edge by a glimmer of tide. Bradley stretches past her and lies down on a patch of flattened grass just below the lip of yard. Leans back on his elbows, crosses his ankles one over the other. He takes Colleen's hand to pull her down next to him. She resists. She wants this to be a stand-up meeting, a face-to-face, but when she remembers how well the tall grass hides them, she concedes and lowers herself to the ground, though she doesn't lie down. She sits apart from him with her knees up and her back straight, leaving enough room for a full-sized person, or a portly Holy Ghost. She tightens her lips. She can see the lab from here.

"Aren't you going to come a little closer?"

Bradley reaches for her but Colleen raises her hand like a traffic cop at a crosswalk and he takes the hint, grinning. Bradley prides himself on his knowledge of women, considers himself a seasoned sailor, able to read women's capricious moods, and tacks patiently. Colleen can be as pin-sharp and prickly as the winter's first hint of sleet, and as changeable as the weather, so he sits back and waits. He is ready to alter his bearings at the slightest shift in the wind. He is curious and excited that she has asked to meet him here. His top ankle jiggles in anticipation. Colleen does not look at him. She watches a vehicle leave the parking lot of the corner store next to the beach and climb the road that bisects the town before pulling into the driveway of a two-storey house with faded blue siding. She does not turn her face toward Bradley as she speaks.

"You can see everything from up here." She delays the moment. Not quite ready to tell him they are finished.

"It's pretty exposed up here, for sure. Maybe we should find somewhere a little more hidden away." He shifts his weight onto the hip closest to her and sidles his top foot towards her. Touches her ankle, ever so gently, with his toe. "We wouldn't want anyone seeing us."

She does not move. A small concession. Colleen is tempted to let Bradley follow his line of thinking all the way through. She lets him drag his foot over her ankle and along her calf. Lets him replace his foot with his hand when he reaches her knee. His hand finds its way up her thigh and between her legs. She leans back as he traces the outline of her labia, through her clothes. She considers stopping him, she is on a time crunch, but sex with Bradley is good, it is very good, and while she knows they are out of time she thinks there might just be enough minutes left to lay down in the grass or to find a little hidey-hole behind the woodpile.

Bradley pulls his fingers away and she looks at him, finally, irritated that he has stopped. He stands and smiles down at her, takes her by the hand and leads her to the woodshed. The ground is soft with sawdust. There is a half cord of wood piled next to the shed, waiting to be chopped. They skirt the splitting log, the axe blade still buried in it. The air smells of resin, and it is spongy and damp underfoot.

The shed is unlocked. Junks of wood are stacked neatly on one wall, like skulls in a catacomb. The room is crowded with tools and garden supplies. Bradley drags a bag of peat moss to one side to make a little room and pushes Colleen into the space it occupied. She is flanked on one side by a shovel and a heavy metal rake and on the other by a lawn mower. Bradley presses his body into hers, presses hard with his hips so that she can feel his erection through their clothes. He takes a step backwards to unbutton his jeans while Colleen slides off her pants, but she puts out a hand to stop him before he can slip his jeans over his hips. Instead, she pulls him close again and pushes down, one hand on his shoulder, the other tangled through his hair. He gives her a shit-eating grin and complies, sinking to the floor. Colleen closes her eyes, her hand on his head while he licks and bites, pulling his hair as she orgasms. Bradley flicks again with his tongue after he knows she has finished and elicits an unexpected scream. He speaks up at her from his knees.

"That's what I like to hear, Doctor."

"Is it?" Colleen answers, labouring to catch her breath.

He reaches up to pull her onto to the plywood floor but she shakes her head. That grin, again, that might belong to the cat with the canary.

"No. You're right. The floor is rotten."

It is rotten. Tracked all over with muddy footprints and splotches of machine oil from the chainsaw and clods of sheep manure. He grabs her hips and uses them to pull himself to standing.

"Don't worry. I got this figured out."

He is quick on his feet. Hitches one hand under her knee and with the other works his boxers and jeans over his hips.

"We haven't tried vertical yet."

But Colleen slips free and sidesteps him, pulling up her cargo pants as she retreats to the middle of the room. Bradley loses his balance, half-dressed. He reaches out a hand to steady himself but grabs the handle of the rake. Stumbles as the rake, and the shovel, too, clatter loudly to the floor. Colleen does not reach out a hand to help him.

"What the hell? What's the matter?"

Bradley looks back over at Colleen with confused eyes. Struggles to stand up straight and fix his clothes at the same time. He cannot quite find his feet in the small space and it is more difficult than it looks to get himself together. Colleen watches him collect himself.

"Nothing is the matter. Look, Bradley." Colleen is business-like. Brusque and efficient, checking her watch as she smooths a hand over the front of her pants. Glancing down to see if the buttons of her shirt are straight. "I don't think I can do this anymore."

She pulls the elastic from her hair and snaps it onto her wrist. Shakes her hair loose, a cascade of strawberry blonde. Her hair falling as straight and heavy as rain on a windless day. In the half light of the shed it glows dully like burnished brass, a glint of red. Bradley watches it settle as if he is Aladdin in the cave watching bolts of silk unfurl, shot through with gold thread. He is bemused and enchanted and perplexed and suddenly agitated. He cannot quite believe what she is saying. He is afraid she is serious.

Colleen smoothes her hair with her palms and pulls it back into a severe ponytail that pulls at her temples. She splits the ponytail into two thick strands and tugs them apart to make sure it is tight.

Bradley studies her face, and snorts out a laugh.

"Christ, I thought for a minute you meant it."

Colleen looks him square in the eye.

"I do mean it. I can't do this anymore."

"You can't do this anymore?" Bradley's voice is all confusion and incredulity. He looks around the room in bewilderment as if searching for answers in the corners, behind the whipper snipper. "What the hell was all that?"

RATS

TAMA opens the screen door carrying a salt beef bucket in one hand. The bucket is overflowing, full of onion and ginger peelings, limp rhubarb leaves hanging over the sides like elephant ears. Insects flit about the patio and the air is alive with sound. She can hear the buzz of mosquitoes and the softer note of wings beating against the glass window. The café is painted dark blue and moths cover the inky clapboard making the wall look like a swath of brocade unfurled against the sky, the fabric pulsating with slowly beating wings. It is throbbing, alive. Tama is quick to latch the door behind her. The last thing she needs is wings and antennae in her jellies, faceted eyes staring out as if preserved in amber, waiting to be spread on toast. Beneath the porch light the floorboards are littered with white-winged corpses, crunchy as autumn leaves under her sneakers.

She descends the steps and crosses the lawn, past the picnic tables and her pots of herbs. The grass is wet with dew.

The night has come in quick and cold, the sun slipping away like a broken egg yolk through her fingers. The summer already showing signs of slipping into fall. She is not wearing socks inside her sneakers and in seconds her ankles are wet. She rounds the corner of the shed and removes the lid of the black plastic compost bin, tips in the contents of her bucket. The bin is nearly full, the top layer of compost littered with grass clippings and coffee grounds. There is a sweet, earthy smell of decay. Earthworms, she knows, are doing their work, boring through apple cores and munching lettuce ends, making black loam of kitchen scraps. She is struggling with the lid, she can never line up the threads, when she freezes. A sound inside the woodshed. The clatter, Tama is sure, of something falling over. The rat.

The rat has been her nemesis the whole winter long and into the summer. It had burrowed through her raised garlic bed, eating every bulb, and when she dug into the bed with her trowel in the spring the soil collapsed into a deep tunnel. The rat had bedded down in the shed and had strewn grass seed and mulch from one end to the other. She'd opened the door in the spring to find chaff mixed with pellets of rat shit the size of foil-wrapped, chocolate Easter eggs. A whole bag of cedar chips wasted. She had swept it all into a garbage bag and thrown it away, breathing in the dusty air, her snot black when she blew her nose later that day.

The rat has studiously ignored the live trap tucked behind the hole gnawed in the compost bin. It has avoided the regular spring trap, baited with peanut butter and a piece of fried egg. Tama has, so far, shied away from setting out poison, she doesn't want it leaching into her vegetables, but she is starting to worry the rat is breeding. She can picture a litter of naked babies, warm and cozy in a den at the bottom of the garden, long tails wrapped around one another.

She gently lays down the lid of the compost bin, trying not to make a sound, considering her options. She would like to bash its head in with a shovel but the shovel is in the shed and she isn't sure if she is prepared to do battle in such a confined space. She certainly cannot go into the shed unarmed. The rat will feel cornered, driven to viciousness. It will stare her down with its red eyes.

She casts around for a big stick. Finds a skinny log on the jumbled woodpile, the bark smooth against her hand, and creeps toward the shed door. And stops. A voice. Voices. She hears voices. Have the rats started talking now? Are they planning a conspiracy?

But of course they are not and in a split second she picks out Bradley's booming tenor. Recognizes his voice, even though it is muffled by the walls, even though her ears seem to be filling with fluid and it is as if she is listening to him from beneath the surface of a swimming pool. The water in her ears is interfering with her equilibrium. She is suddenly dizzy and reaches out a hand to steady herself, the smooth surface of the compost bin warm under her palm. She freezes in place like one of those buskers who hold their position for hours, she had seen them once in Leicester Square, and you could never be sure if they were bronze or flesh until you reached out your finger to touch them and they turned to look right at you and you jumped back with a little scream.

She cannot quite pick out words, though the tones are as

clear as the notes on a piano. Tama can hear Bradley entreating, supplicating, his voice growing louder, more highly pitched before retreating again. She has heard this refrain before—Bradley pleading with her not to go, to stay, he needs her, he can't live without her. She knows this song by heart. The second voice carries a more insistent, straightforward melody—a line from a military march maybe. Something definite and final. Tama follows the musical arc of the conversation—the tune gaining in pitch and volume, crescendoing to a climax.

And then it is over. A final cadence that resolves every argument, and in the sudden silence Tama snaps out of her stupor. She scurries to flatten herself against the side of the shed, hiding out with the rats, as if in ambush, though in reality she doesn't want to be seen. She waits while the door squeaks open and squeaks shut again. Gives the pair in the shed time to cross the grassy lawn before peeking around the corner. Bradley stands slope-shouldered, hands in his pockets, his eyes on the lanky figure striding along the edge of the property almost, but not quite, hidden in the shadow of the trees. As if Colleen's precautions are now beside the point, as if she has already put this entire episode with Bradley out of her mind, and is stalking off into the future.

Tama knows it will be hours before she sees Bradley. He will shoot her a text, he is reaching for his phone as he slopes across the driveway. He will take a late night walk and end up at the wharf watching the moon on the bay. Creep home in the wee hours and have a drink or two at the kitchen table—something strong. Liquor not beer. He will sneak into their bedroom, drop his clothes to the floor and lift the blankets ever so softly. Crawl naked into bed and curl up next to her. Pull her body tight to his, one hand on her breast as he falls asleep. Tama drops the junk of wood she is holding into the grass. She has gripped it so tightly that she has burst a sap bubble with her fingernails. Her hands are sticky and smell of trees.

SINKING

VIVIENNE is sitting on a chair pulled up to the side of the freezer, her head resting on her forearms. With one hand she traces figure eights in the murky water causing evanescent eddies that vanish as soon as she pulls away her fingertips, literal tempests that could fit in a teacup. She has spent the evening peering into the tank. The creature has moved occasionally, taking sluggish circuits of its cell, but these episodes are brief. Mostly she sinks into what seem to be long stretches of sleep or unconsciousness. Still, Vivienne is relieved to see the fish move, as slumberous as she is. She is assured, for the moment, that the creature hasn't slipped into a coma. That she isn't dead.

The creature has stopped eating and her face is gaunt. Vivienne had returned from the run in the boat with a handful of live crabs. She had thrown them into the freezer when Colleen left to meet Isaiah, but the creature refused to touch them. The crabs, sensing the predator above them, scrambled to press themselves as far into the corners as they were able, searching in vain for a rock or a sprig of seaweed to hide behind. But it had not taken long for them to perceive the creature's weakness, and instead of trying to secret themselves away, they stalked purposefully across the bottom of the tank, as self-assured as a flight of flamenco dancers. When they began nipping at the flesh of the creature's tail with their pincers Vivienne had been forced to find a fishing net and scoop them out.

It has been only a matter of days since the fish commenced her hunger strike but already the architecture of her skeletal system is showing through her skin, the elegant bony frame of her shoulders and tail, the cantilevered spread of her ribs. Vivienne pulls the book she borrowed from the library in Carbonear from her backpack and spreads it across her lap. Opens it to the ink drawing she has marked with a slip of paper and compares anatomies. Wonders if the drawing is an artist's fancy, a picture made of made-up stories, or an accurate reportage on a contemporary dissection.

When she was healthier, the creature swam nearly incessantly but there were moments of stillness which would, without fail, lure Vivienne to the tank. The sudden absence of the faint sound caused by the fish's motion would lift Vivienne from her seat at the workbench to see if she was alright, the silence flooding her ears. She approached the tank first with worry and then trepidation and finally dread. The creature would be lying in wait, her tail wound tight as a silver spring and Vivienne was amazed she could make herself so small. Her sinewy arms pressed against the flat bottom of the freezer, tense with muscle and ready to spring upwards and attack. Her seaweed appendages drifting in the lazy current, a perfect blind to hide behind. Vivienne could see just how the adaption would work in the cool dark of a sea cave or in the dappled sunlight of the open ocean floor. Delicate ribbons fluttering, the creature coiled in ambush.

In one of these fraught, still moments the undulating seaweed had obscured the creature's face and Vivienne had shone a flashlight into the tank, the beam perfectly simulating sunlight through salt water. In the gloom of the store, the fish's arms had appeared mottled, her scaly skin sparking with brilliance. She caught the creature's eye as she peeked through her false forest and found herself overcome with emotion, ashamed and heartsick. She moved the flashlight away, then, angling the beam toward the ceiling. Catching in its glare dust motes floating like plankton in the column of light as she slid to the floor, back against the white tank. Tears leaking between her squeezed-shut eyelids.

Now the fish is leaden, her face buried in the corner, her animal rage drained away. Her arms float loosely, as if they have been dislocated from her shoulders. As if they are driftwood caught in a mass of kelp, so much flotsam and jetsam. Her inertia unnerves Vivienne who expects her, still, to lunge at her, teeth bared.

Vivienne keeps watch as the fish sleeps or suffers or dreams, heart skipping every time she surfaces into semi-consciousness. She watches and croons throughout the long night. Tells the creature all her secret hurts—about Eliza and her broken, broken heart, about Isaiah and Colleen and her fear and confusion, about the desperate fog of loneliness in which she is engulfed. She says to the fish: squeeze my hand if you can hear me. Reaches out and uncurls the delicate appendage that is folded like a fist, like origami, uncrumpling it gently with her fingers. She holds it until her own hand is numbed by the frigid water, the slender phalanges still limp. When the creature's face floats free of the corner, Vivienne reaches down to grasp the fish's chin. She says: blink once for yes, twice for no. But the reptilian eyelids—double-lidded and dull—do not blink. Eyes nubilous, pupils dilated. Her face is slippery and Vivienne cannot keep a grip on her jawbone. Sleep is very far away.

SANDWICHES
AND A THERMOS
OF COFFEE

TAMA has fallen asleep in front of the TV, curled up in a crazy quilt her nan had made, watching an old movie in the dark—something with Gene Kelly and a very young Frank Sinatra. They are in the navy; they are tap dancing on the beds. She has dozed off, and Bradley wakes her as he sneaks in, but she lies quietly with her eyes closed as he passes. The credits roll up the screen and an up-tempo jazz number plays as he brushes his teeth and flushes the toilet, eases shut the bedroom door. She has slept through the ending and will never find out who gets the girl.

Sleep ruined, she heads to the café kitchen to get a head start on the day's baking. The air grows yeasty as she beats down the dough and shapes it with her fingers, fitting three rounded mounds into each pan. She snaps on the radio and washes the few dishes she has used while she waits for the bread to bake. Sits and stares out the window until the bread smells done. She pops the loaves out of the oven and raps each loaf with her knuckles to hear if they sound hollow. Slips them out of their pans and slathers each one with butter while it is still hot, wax paper crinkly beneath fingertips so calloused they no longer feel the heat. When half a dozen loaves stand cooling on metal racks, crusty and glistening, she looks first at the clock and then out the window. The green pickup has not moved from its spot next to the rented bungalow.

The truck has become a thing she can't help but see. Her eye seems automatically drawn to it, the way she might hone in on a nearly invisible stain on her shirt that only she would ever notice. Colleen had parked the truck at the house earlier, before she'd ventured over to rendezvous with Bradley in Tama's garden shed. Thinking, no doubt, she was the height of discretion for leaving it behind. Sauntering right up the middle of the road when she'd left, for anyone sitting on their chesterfield watching the late news to see. Tama can see into the kitchen of the bungalow, the blinds have not been lowered, and she has been watching Colleen and Isaiah most of the night, as they sit and talk and peck at the computer and stand to stretch, but now the light has been switched off. The clock reads 3:13.

Bradley has not emerged from the bedroom to ask when she is coming to bed. She can imagine him curled up on the mattress in the fetal position, dejected and cold, too miserable to get up and find an extra blanket. Tama pulls on a hoodie with VENICE written across the front in white block letters, and packs a paper bag. There is still over an hour until she opens for the day.

Just inside the plank door of the store, Vivienne is struggling with a navy windbreaker, the padlock that will lock her into the store from the inside looped over one finger. She had been out for a smoke and had pulled the windbreaker on over her sweater to keep off the damp. It is made of some kind of crinkly material that makes a sound like cellophane. She wonders if it is nylon or polyester or some space-age synthetic that repels water and protects against UVA rays and UVB rays and is probably Wi-Fi capable. Maybe it is Kevlar. Whatever it is, it is loud in her ears. The coat is noisy and it is too big and she wonders who it belongs to, it certainly isn't hers. She is almost sure it is Colleen's and tries to picture the jacket on her. She thinks it must be the one Colleen wears while she waits on the wharf in the early morning hours for Vivienne to pull up in the punt, the one she grabs when there is a drizzle of rain and they are popping over to the café for lunch. She can almost hear the jacket crinkle as Colleen shifts gears in the truck. She is almost certain.

Still, the windbreaker is anonymous-looking, it could be anyone's windbreaker, and she is anxious to get it off. It feels as if it is smothering her, closing off her windpipe. Maybe she's been smoking too much. Maybe she's smoked herself out. Maybe tobacco smoke or nicotine or some other cigarette poison has seeped into the fabric of the jacket and is interacting with the space-age material and she is being gassed. Probably it is the tar. Or the formaldehyde.

She is abruptly, overwhelmingly hot and tries to rip the windbreaker off her body, but she pulls at the zipper so violently it catches at the fabric and becomes stuck an inch or so from the collar. She thinks if she can only get the toggle down a little bit further she will be able to pull the whole coat down over her hips and step out of it. She is nearly in tears and she slips the padlock still looped over her finger into a pocket so she has full use of her hands and she grasps the zip and pulls and, just as abruptly as it had seized up, it releases and slides down as easy as butter. She peels the jacket from her arms and flings it at the nail where it usually hangs. It catches and hangs there askew, looking like last summer's scarecrow, a scarecrow coming down in the wind, the kind of scarecrow birds would laugh at on their way to a feed of seed. She is weak with relief to be coatless. She feels as though her legs can barely hold her and she coopies down, one hand on the floor, before she falls over.

And this is how Tama finds her: Vivienne's face bloated and red, splotchy from the cry she'd allowed herself earlier, and sweaty from the fight with the jacket. Squat down on the floor. Vivienne does not hear the door creak open. And when she senses the person standing over her, she looks up as if she is an animal caught. Vivienne has to tilt her head upwards to see Tama fully from her position on the floor, apparated from nowhere wearing hiking boots and carrying a brown paper bag. Later she will wonder if her bout with the jacket is the reason she did not hear Tama creak the door open. She will wonder why she did not, at the very least, first hook the arm of the padlock through the loop.

Vivienne feels as if she has become rooted but while her body remains immobile, her mind moves backward in time. She is sitting in Intro to Oceanic Invertebrates, the class is covering the unit on bivalves. She can feel the soft seat of the lecture hall under her legs, can feel the Formica desktop cool against her wrist. She is watching a PowerPoint presentation, the word *sessile* taking up the full screen. She remembers the high voice of the prof, who had come to class always in a pair of green rubber boots, the way he had lisped over the word. He clicked to the next slide and read out the definition. *Sessile: An organism attached directly to a fixed object via a stalk; i.e., barnacles, corals, bivalves.*

The sight of Tama has rendered Vivienne sessile. She is a mollusk, a mussel, clinging to a sea-battered rock, except the rock is the salt-stained wooden floor of the store and the sea is the whisper of wind through the astoundingly open doorway. The fact of Tama, with her sturdy boots and her parcel, sends every ounce of Vivienne's blood rushing, circumnavigating her body like a gyre. The tidal pull that might erode rock faces cannot move her, she is held in place despite the undertow. How terrifying to be a bivalve, unable to slam their shell shut against impending disaster. Watching catastrophe descend upon them. Vivienne is gaping, all her tender flesh exposed.

When Tama speaks, she speaks as if there is nothing out of the ordinary, as if she finds nothing strange in discovering Vivienne, sweaty and red, crouched on the floor of the store.

First: "Sandwiches. And a thermos of coffee. You came straight to work after I saw you and I wasn't sure you'd had a chance to eat." The hour spent swinging their legs in the oak tree at the top of the hill seems very far away.

And then, responding to the undissipated look of panic on Vivienne's face: "It's not as bad as all that, is it, girl?"

Tama lays down the bag, a line of concern drawn between her eyebrows. She takes a step towards Vivienne.

Takes both Vivienne's hands in hers and pulls her to her feet. They stand. Tama does not let go of her. She is saying, "Take your time, girl. Take your time." Crooning at her like a feral kitten. Vivienne considers her options. A rent has opened, an unexpected opportunity has presented itself.

Vivienne's thoughts become loose and unmoored and she finds herself caught in a daydream like a fish in a net. She imagines she is swimming, imagines slipping beneath the waves. She can feel the shock of water on skin, the sting of salt biting into the abrasions along her spine that have yet to heal—she is still sore and bloody, the scabs pulling loose at night in her sleep as she sails on sea-tossed dreams. She can smell brine. She can feel the skim of warm water at the surface, can touch the beginnings of the frigid depths with her toes. She can see the play of sun in the water.

"Tama, what am I going to do?"

"Vivienne." Tama speaks gently. She is about to say: This girl. I know you love her. But you will find someone else to love. There is someone else out there who will love you. Instead she tilts her head and looks at Vivienne consideringly. "This isn't about Eliza, is it?"

At Tama's question Vivienne's mind snaps back to the store. In the long moment they have stood holding hands, the thought of Eliza has not crossed her mind. She is unsure how to answer. When she finally speaks, her words are as faint as a clam opening its shell. "Tama, can I show you something?"

She walks backwards, still holding Tama's hands. They are like two children dancing. Vivienne leads Tama across the floor, stops when her back touches the freezer. She drops her hands to touch Tama's waist and manoeuvres her so that they face each other, hips touching the tank. She looks Tama in the eye, holding her gaze as if with string, as if with some indissoluble filament.

"In here. She's in here."

Vivienne looks into the freezer, snipping the thread between. Tama follows her gaze. The creature appears lifeless. Her body has floated upwards. Tama reaches out to find Vivienne's fingers, twining them gently through her own. If Tama and Vivienne have been children, dancing across the wooden floor, the fish is a child playing at drowning. Her face submerged, shoulders floating while her tail sinks to scrape the bottom of the tank. Her kelpy appendages making it appear as though she is entangled in a mass of seaweed. The flutter of gills the only whisper of motion.

Tama inhales, the sound not quite a gasp. Her voice, when she finally speaks, is soft, as if she is frightened of waking her. "Is she alive?" she asks. And, "Do you know what she is?"

Vivienne tells her the story of blue moonbeams on the sea and swarms of jellyfish and the jagged hook, of the bumpy road to the store and the poor man's fish tank and the tests. The nibbling crabs. This floating stillness. She tells her almost everything.

The coffee is still hot inside the thermos. Vivienne and Tama sip at steaming cups, Vivienne's a slurry of sugar and cream. They pull two chairs against the side of the freezer, facing each other. Vivienne unwraps a sandwich from its wax paper;

the relief of spilling her story to Tama has left her famished. The release overwhelming. She feels emptied, her head and heart lighter. There is space again in her brain, her liver, her gut. She drains her cup, tucks into the lunch Tama has prepared.

"The plan," says Vivienne, "is to move her to St. John's. The next day or two I think? But I honestly don't know if she'll make it that long. She's worse every minute."

"Do you think she'll do any better in town? This thing," Tama knocks a knuckle against the tank, "is beyond ridiculous, but whatever kind of set-up they have in there, it's still not going to be the ocean. What makes them think they can keep her alive in there any better than they can out here?"

"They don't know. They have no idea what they're doing, no matter what they might pretend." Vivienne has inhaled the sandwich. She crumples the wax paper and rolls it into a ball, squeezing it until the wrapper is as small as a marble. The coffee and the food have fortified her. She feels stronger, more clear-eyed than she has in days. She brushes the crumbs from her lap. Places the ball of wax paper in her cup and lays the cup on the floor.

She reaches into the freezer and untangles the creature's hand from the ribbons of kelp. The hand appears lifeless, the bony digits limp, and she kneads them as if trying to rub warmth back into frostbitten fingers. She knows what will happen to her if she doesn't survive the trip to St. John's. Vivienne has seen birds and fish and sea mammals—seals and even a porpoise—dissected. She imagines the scalpel carving a line from the fish's throat to her belly. Imagines watching as her organs are cut free from her body, she can feel the weight of them in her gloved hands. She imagines the colony of Dermestid beetles feasting on the remaining flesh, cleaning her bones for display. She can hear the sound of them devouring her.

Vivienne looks into the murky water and weighs the harm that has been done to the creature's body. Nearly all her scales have come loose now, leaving behind skin textured with flaky scabs. She traces the filigreed veins at the creature's wrist with her fingertip, and the delicate scaffold of bones. Strokes the creature's flank. She is considering the delicate intricacy of her circulatory system, envisioning it spiderwebbing beneath a paper-thin layer of skin when, unexpectedly, a spasm ripples through her muscular tail. For an instant Vivienne feels a tremor of suppressed power. The convulsion is enough to shake her off and she jumps back, her shirt splattered with water.

"Oh!" Tama jumps back off her chair, knocking it over, her coffee spilling to the floor. The splash has hit her full in the face, her hair is dripping. "What was that?" Wiping water from her eyes. "She's unconscious. She's been unconscious these two days."

"Is she now?"

But a new thought is already occurring to Vivienne. She takes up the limp wrist again, feels for a pulse. She can feel the throb of blood, muted but definite. She peers more closely at the fish's ravaged skin. Vivienne had once inherited an orchid from a roommate. The plant had been unspectacular, a mat of tongue-like leaves and one gangly shoot. But the shoot had sprouted a handful of green buds and each bud had sent out a blossom, the orchid blooming as yellow as an egg

MELISSA BARBEAU

181

yolk. Vivienne scrutinizes a single scab. Beneath the crusty abrasion, a jade green lamina, like a bud on her lanky orchid, peeps out. New growth. She thinks about the schools of herring feeding on the banks of algae lighting up the sea— flashing silver and leaving her nets clogged, shedding scales like the leaves of a deciduous tree to more easily escape their predators.

The creature is once more immobile, seemingly insensible, seemingly unaware. As if the flick was an anomaly. As if it hadn't happened at all.

Vivienne pictures the brown rabbits she often comes across on the wooded path behind the university. Hares, really, with enormous feet and ears. She surprises them sometimes, if she rounds a corner quietly and they are absorbed in nibbling at a leafy twig, and they freeze in fright. Too terrified to move.

She makes a decision.

"Tama, can you help me? I need you to create a diversion."

THE PHONE
RINGS SIX TIMES

THE phone rings six times before it is picked up.

"Newsroom. Ben Sharpe speaking."

BOLD AS
BRASS AND TAKING
NUMBERS

MORNING dawns bright. The day large. Tama has propped the door of the café open with a beach rock as large as a tomcat to let in the sunshine. She hears the green truck through the open doorway before she sees it. It has developed a clunk. Tama is no expert on green trucks, or at least she wasn't an expert on green trucks until this summer when she became the world's leading authority on one particular green truck, but even she knows the vehicle is sick. She can hear it coming from miles away. It is the exhaust—something has come loose. Years ago, Tama owned an ailing Honda Civic. She had hit a pothole coming out of downtown St. John's, knocking one end of the exhaust pipe from the undercarriage and had driven all the way to Kingsbridge Auto with the muffler dragging on the asphalt, sparks spitting. Cringing as she passed the Dominion, people at the bus stop staring as she drove by. The green truck is making the same foreboding noises as the luckless Civic—it sounds like an animal labouring. A nag ready for the glue factory, asthmatic and loud, bellowing its way up the hill. She hears the truck groan in existential disbelief, as if it cannot believe it is being asked to make it all the way to the café.

Colleen pulls onto the gravel lot and turns off the vehicle. The windows must be rolled down, Tama can hear Isaiah talking as soon as the engine dies. He is loud. His mouth going a mile a minute, hardly stopping for breath. He is talking too fast, there are too many words coming out of his mouth and Tama can tell even from the dining room that he is operating on a manic setting. They get out and she hears the car doors, one after the other. Thunk. Thunk. Colleen jangles her keys as they clomp up the steps, Isaiah still talking, talking, talking.

They blink the sun from their eyes as they enter, standing in the open doorway as their pupils adjust. It is Sunday and the kind of morning that will bring people to the cove on day trips. It is not quite noon and there are already customers in the café, it's looking to be a busy lunch hour. There is a party of tourists with cameras huddled over a stack of glossy pamphlets. A single male traveller with a map fanned out in front of him. The man has ordered coffee and blueberry pie with ice cream for lunch. He is vocal in his enjoyment of the pie—he has already suggested ordering a second piece. Two couples sit together at the table beside the window, barely speaking, barely looking at one another. They are in the area, they tell Tama glumly, for a funeral further down the shore. Someone's aunt. Not the way they had planned on spending their day.

Colleen studies the choice of seating. The bigger tables

are taken and she and Isaiah are forced to sit at a smaller two-person setting. The arrangements are cozier than she would like. There is no space to spread out their books and devices and other ephemera. No way to have a truly private conversation. They are on top of each other, knees clunking together.

Colleen nods at Tama and heads to the back. She grabs a cup from a hook and half fills it, emptying the coffee pot. Shakes the empty pot at Tama and turns without waiting for Tama's response.

"We're going to put in an order when you're ready," Isaiah shouts jovially. His high spirits bounce around the room. Tama nods as she puts a fresh pot of coffee to brew. He is loud enough to attract attention, his excitement palpable. The two couples at the window stare at him morosely. Bradley pokes his head briefly out the kitchen at the sound of his voice. Retreats just as quickly, his neck retracting through the doorway like a turtle withdrawing into its shell.

"Can you grab them real quick?" Tama speaks loudly enough for Bradley to hear her from his lookout position inside the door. She indicates Colleen and Isaiah's table with a nod and turns on the tap at the bar to rinse out the coffeepot. The sound of running water drowns out Bradley's answer. He tries again as Tama places the carafe on the burner.

"No can do. I'm right in the middle of something in here." He peeks around the doorframe into the dining room. Colleen is sitting with her back to him and doesn't turn around. Still, he reddens.

"What are you doing that's so urgent? We haven't got an order up. Can you please help me out here and see what they want to eat?" Tama is puttering around the coffee station. "I have to grind beans." She is opening the big Tupperware container and pouring coffee beans into the stainless steel grinder. "Go on now." Bradley emerges reluctantly. He eases his apron over his head and grabs a notebook and pencil off the counter.

"Hey, there. What'll you have?" All business. "Bacon and eggs for you, I guess?"

Colleen looks straight across the table at Isaiah as she speaks.

"We're on the clock today. Maybe soup and sandwiches." She looks at her watch. "We shouldn't lollygag too long."

"Nonsense. We've got time." Isaiah is studying the menu blurbs intently. "How's the fish? The pan-fried?" And he is off on a tangential set of questions about battering and breading and oils and seasonings and sides and substitutes for sides and whether the tartar sauce is homemade.

Bradley stands frozen, as if he is a statue of a waiter. As if he's acting out *waiter* in a game of charades, pen poised over pad, writing down nothing. He answers Isaiah's cod-related questions automatically. Studies Colleen's hands until she glances up and realizes what he is doing and slides them onto her lap. She looks anywhere but at him and then twists, her hand on the back of her chair. And even from her position behind the bar, Tama can see that Bradley is looking down Colleen's shirt. She is sure Colleen's movement is purposeful, she is arching her back just a little, pushing her breasts forward, and Bradley is staring fixedly, flagrantly. His face as red and bright as a pin cherry. Tama's heart lurches at his blatancy. She is sick. Sick at Bradley's stupidity almost as much at his betrayal. She almost pities him his stupidity. How can he not see that Colleen is playing with him? That she is stringing him along?

Tama catches Colleen's eye. Colleen can see that Tama has drawn some conclusions but she doesn't miss a beat. She doesn't have time for this shit today. "Coffee ready yet?"

"Brewing. Six minutes."

Colleen turns back to the table. The spell over Bradley broken.

"I'll get this on the stove." He heads to the kitchen without looking back.

Tama busies herself wiping glasses and pulls the carafe from the coffee machine before it has quite finished the brew cycle. The last drops hiss and spatter as they bounce off the heating plate. She approaches their table and reaches for Colleen's half-filled cup. Colleen stops her, places her hand over the top of the mug before Tama has a chance to pour.

"Can I have a fresh cup. This one is cold."

Tama takes a full breath before answering. "Absolutely."

"Make it two." Isaiah's voice bouncy as he holds up two fingers. He is speaking when Tama returns to the table with two mugs hooked over her thumb. "Explain to me again about the oxygenation unit."

Tama fills Isaiah's cup.

"They're being difficult, is the gist of it. Impossible really. But it's hard to impress the importance of getting a delivery immediately—on the weekend, especially—without explaining what you're doing. God forbid you make something a priority just because you're told to."

"So, tomorrow for sure then. We're not going to be able to move it before then."

Tama's hand freezes.

"Today is looking impossible. And Gerry from the lab is camping this weekend. Refuses to come in and get things straightened away. Playing the *union* card. As if this is the only time he'll get to camp in his life. Cup of coffee?" Colleen glances up at Tama. Indicates her cup with a sweep of her hand. "Please?" This is said without politeness. Said, instead, with a heavy flush of sarcasm.

"Sorry, just drifted away for a minute." Tama fills Colleen's cup. There is a clattering noise from the kitchen. It sounds as if Bradley has dropped something. The coffee pot drifts and a trickle of liquid hits Colleen's moleskin notebook, open in front of her on the table.

"Careful! Christ, Tama."

"I'm so sorry." Tama swipes at the wet page with a cloth. Blue ink smears across the page.

"I've got it." Colleen snatches the book away.

"No worries. No worries." Isaiah reassures both women good-naturedly as he hands Colleen a handful of serviettes. She dabs at the notebook furiously. He glances at Tama and winks. "She's got everything card catalogued in that head of hers anyway. This project is not going off the rails over a drop of coffee."

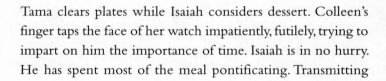

Tama clears plates while Isaiah considers dessert. Colleen's finger taps the face of her watch impatiently, futilely, trying to impart on him the importance of time. Isaiah is in no hurry. He has spent most of the meal pontificating. Transmitting plans between bites of fish as if he were an on-air radio station. Colleen's responses barely audible, though the half conversation Tama has been able to hear has been illuminating.

The funeral party at the window and the tourists with their stack of leaflets have already left as Isaiah dabs at his lips with a napkin and throws it onto the tablecloth. The man with the hiking guides stands and stretches, tidying his maps into a neat pile, raising one finger to Tama to indicate he wants the bill. He seems intent on being friendly and speaks across the room to Colleen and Isaiah as he zips his coat.

"You two seem like regulars. You live out this way?"

Colleen says nothing, but Isaiah, eager to spread his enthusiasm in every direction, turns his chair to face him completely.

"I just got in a couple of days ago but Colleen here is a summer local. She's been out here since the beginning of June."

"Wow. Is that so? I hardly ever get out of the city—the old nine to five and all that. You sure are lucky to manage it. Colleen is it? Sorry," he wipes his hand down the leg of his pants and leans across the table to shake hands. "I'm hardly fit." Isaiah takes his hand but Colleen only nods. She picks up her phone and begins scrolling. Tama is ringing up the bill. "And you're?"

"John Isaiah."

"Nice to meet you, John. You're working in St. John's? Just slipping up here with the wife on the weekends?" He includes Colleen in his glance.

"Ha ha! Nothing like that." Isaiah seems genuinely tickled that this stranger imagines he and Colleen might be a couple. "We're hardly matched, are we? No. All work, I'm afraid. We're connected with the Ocean Sciences Centre at the university. Working on a research project. Studying the glowing tides that have been spotted up here."

"I heard about that. There were some pictures on Instagram. Think there's a chance I might see them if I stay the night?" He turns and looks at Tama. "Is there a B&B in town? Anywhere I can rent a room?" He turns back to Isaiah without waiting for an answer. "I bet you see all kinds of interesting things out there. Out on the ocean all the time."

"Oh, you wouldn't believe." Isaiah is playing smug. Playing the Cheshire Cat.

"Well, that sounds like a yes." The man is all boyish enthusiasm. "I'm crazy for all those Nature Channel specials. What have you seen?"

"I tell you what." Isaiah playing the part of a TV host. Teasing the next episode. "You just watch the news the next couple of weeks. Remember you were talking to me."

Colleen shuts the screen on her phone. Caps her pen. "John. I think we have to get going."

"She keeps me honest, this one."

"Well, that's just the thing." The man takes the credit card terminal from Tama. He continues speaking, ignoring the digression from Colleen. "It seems news that you've found something has preceded you." He juggles the terminal to pull a business card from his pocket, reaching over the table between them to hand it to Isaiah. "I'm Ben Sharpe. I'm with the *Independent*."

"The *Independent*?" Genuine confusion crosses Isaiah's face. "Of *London*?"

Ben Sharpe laughs. "I wish. Of Newfoundland."

"You're a newspaper."

"That's right. I received a call about a discovery down here." He opens a notebook, consults his notes. "And I think you've just confirmed it."

Isaiah blanches. The silence is monumental. Colleen lays down her phone. She grips the edge of the table and Tama thinks she might flip it over or fling it like a discus at Ben Sharpe or use it to leverage herself off her chair and bolt for the door.

"John Isaiah. And Colleen. Do you have a last name, Colleen? And do either of you have a comment?" He pulls out his cellphone, finds the audio recorder. "Or." He waits, as if considering. As if these thoughts are just occurring to him. "We could make an appointment. A more formal arrangement, you might say. A proper sit down. We could even do it here, the food is excellent. It is." He turns to include Tama, standing at his elbow with the credit card terminal, in the conversation.

Tama looks from person to person as the silence ticks by. Isaiah leaning forward, hands on his knees. Colleen vise-gripped to the table. Ben Sharpe standing with his phone outstretched. The players form a frozen tableau or a strange Renaissance painting. It is Colleen that breaks loose. She stands, snatches the business card from Isaiah's fingers.

"Come on."

"How did you know?" Isaiah's eyes are big. Tama sees that he is speaking thoughts as they come to his mind, that they are exiting his mouth unfiltered. She can see the effort Colleen is making to get Isaiah out of the café. Tama thinks that at any moment she will lift him up bodily and fling him over her shoulder. "Who told you?"

Colleen interrupts. "I think what Dr. Isaiah means is we are unsure where you may have gotten this so-called information. There's nothing to confirm."

"The source is really unimportant at the moment. And let's be upfront here. We have a monthly newspaper. We would like to do a feature article. Coincide its release with whatever press conference or announcement you have planned." Ben Sharpe spreads his hands magnanimously. "But we also have a web presence. It is possible to write something up quickly and run with it from there." He shakes his head, as if dismissing this idea. As if he cannot believe anyone would be foolish enough to force this option.

Isaiah's voice is quiet. The bombastic tone he had used earlier to address the room has escaped through an open window. "I don't understand. No one knows about it. Did you call anyone?" He turns to address Colleen. "Who have you been talking to?"

"What I would like to do is sit down. Maybe have a meal together. We can do this in a way that is mutually beneficial to everyone." Sharpe's voice reasonable and measured. "This is a scoop, Dr. Isaiah. And a scoop is a rare thing in this day and age. I'm afraid I'm going to have to insist that we negotiate terms."

"Did I call anyone? Why in the hell would I do that?" Colleen smooths the lines that have appeared on her fore-head. Tama can see the headache forming behind her eyes, can see it marching with migraine steps into her brain. Colleen rubs her eyes as if she might scrub them from her head. "I called no one. But I fucking know who might have."

"Who? The girl?" Isaiah is genuinely confused. "I took care of her."

"Did you now?"

"I did." He sounds definite. Defensive.

"Fuck, Isaiah. This is not the place to have this conversation. We have to leave."

"You'll be in touch?" Ben Sharpe has watched the exchange between them intently.

Colleen addresses Tama. "I'll swing round and pay the bill later." She does not wait for Tama's reply. She is pulling Isaiah from his chair by the wrist.

"That's quite the vehicle you have out there." Ben Sharpe's voice still friendly as he speaks to their retreating backs. "Looks like she's been through the war."

Colleen stops mid-step.

"I think I'll drop by for a cup of tea after supper. You put the kettle on and I'll bring a sweet. You're staying up the hill over there, right? The blue house with the new deck? Or I can meet you at your work station down in the cove. Or here?"

"Closed for supper," Tama says.

"Too bad. Alright, I'll track you down by the truck, what do you say? Pop by around eight?" He is folding his receipt carefully and placing it in his wallet, probably claiming lunch as an expense when he gets back to St. John's. He strolls out the door, one hand in his jeans pocket, checking messages on his phone as he goes.

Colleen and Isaiah wait until his car pulls away. Then she is dragging him from the café, she has his sleeve bunched in one fist, she is shoving him into the passenger side of the vehicle and slamming his door. Tama is bussing the table when she sees Colleen's notebook. She makes to chase after her and is nearly bowled over at the door when Colleen comes back for it.

Colleen pushes past her before Tama has a chance to speak. "Colleen."

"What?"

"You left this." Tama holds the notebook just out of reach.

Colleen knocks against her and snatches it from her hand. "Thanks."

"You're lucky it was me picked it up and not that guy you were arguing with." She holds Colleen's gaze. "You've been careless these past few days. Leaving all kinds of things laying out in the open."

"I don't know what you're talking about."

"No, I suppose not."

Bradley comes out of the kitchen as Colleen pounds down the stairs. The truck pulls out of the lot, engine revving, Colleen's fury transmitting itself through the way she stomps on the gas pedal. The vehicle responds desperately, struggling to keep up with her rage as they squeal up the road. Bradley wipes his hands on his apron. Tama is the first to speak.

"You barely said hello to that crowd this morning?" It is not really a question. More an observation.

"No." He is stacking plates, laying cutlery on top of them.

"Hiding away in the kitchen." Another not-question.

"I'm a bit off this morning. Not feeling quite right."

"Oh." She wipes the table as he clears away the dishes. "Over indulged a little last night, maybe? You were late coming in."

"No. I wasn't drinking. Just feeling low, I guess." He takes a deep breath. "You know how it is. Days you wonder if we made the right decision trying to make a go of it out here."

Bradley gives a ghost of his sparkling smile. His eyes sad. Tama feels sick, a wave of bile roils in her stomach. She feels an urge at the back of her throat. She is afraid she will vomit.

It had been Bradley's suggestion to move back here from Europe, to give this outport restaurant thing a try. He had seen the restaurant advertised online. Damson Bay, what are the chances? Tama's hometown. Currently operating as a fish and chips place, he read, but you could convert it, the set up is already there. And they already had a name: what could be better than Atwater's Café for a place by the sea. He kept adding reasons like stringing beads on a length of thread. There's more and more tourists up this way every year. Art studios and tours to all those resettled communities and the boat museum is only over the barrens. They could make a go of it. Do the gastro café thing.

The truth of it was, though, that it was more about the girl who lived in the flat across the hall than a business opportunity. A smart *bibliothécaire* Tama was sure he was sleeping with. He had been heartbroken when they'd caught her in a tangly embrace in the lift. The elegant librarian had giggled and blushed but the tall man she was with had grinned and said a cheerful *Bonjour* before lifting her long hair to kiss the nape of her neck. Not long after, Bradley, full up on long walks in the rain, had told Tama he was homesick. Had pointed out the ad for the café. Tama shakes her head in irritation at the memory. She is suddenly fuming that he is second-guessing their decision to move back, that he is so easily throwing away this second chance.

But her voice, when she answers him, betrays none of her anger. Instead, she coats her words in a thick syrup of wifely concern.

"You can't get discouraged." She fiddles with the dishrag in her hand. "Things get hard. You have to go after what you want. You can't let anyone discourage you if you're sure."

Bradley is looking at her now. Considering. "Maybe."

"Your advice for the day." She takes the dirty plates from his hands and heads to the kitchen and then stops as if just remembering something. "Oh. I'm going to get you to pop over some coffee to the research crowd later. I was doing a little eavesdropping. Sounds like they might be extending their stay. It would be nice to encourage their business if they're going to be around into the fall."

She does not turn around to see his reaction.

A FABLE

S HE is sitting at the work bench when Colleen and Isaiah bang into the store. There is no time left. Isaiah does not move from the open doorway, but Colleen strides towards Vivienne, her boots on the wooden floor booming like cannons. Her face masked in anger.

"Get up." Colleen is as imperious as a queen in a Shakespearean tragedy, passing sentence on Vivienne's head. The light from the open doorway hits her like a spotlight. "I don't know what you're playing at but you are finished. That phone call was over the line." Her voice ringing with finality.

"What phone call?"

"What call?" Colleen's hands on her hips, her body still. Isaiah is shaking with rage. His face the colour of the ball in a mercury thermometer, his blood boiling. He is shaking with emotion.

"Give me your keys." Colleen extends her hand. "Get out, get out, get out," she intones, "and don't look back."

"But." The freezer glows like a sun at the edge of Vivienne's periphery. "How am I getting back to town?"

"Are you kidding me? You want a ride? Holy hell, Vivienne. Get out of my sight."

Vivienne edges towards the creature. She is wondering if she can scoop her out of the tank. Hoist her over her shoulder and run.

"Oh no." Colleen seems to grow taller. She steps in front of Vivienne, blocking her from reaching the freezer. "You can forget it. Keys. Now." Vivienne digs them from the pocket of her shorts and places them on Colleen's outstretched palm.

Isaiah stands on the threshold as she exits.

"Excuse me. Please."

But he holds his place, nearly blocking the door, and she is forced to squeeze past him. Her skin crawls everywhere her body touches his, as if covered in red ants.

She heads straight to the café. Goes round to the back door, hoping to find Tama in the kitchen. Instead it is Bradley standing by the stove, assembling sandwiches. "Tama's in the dining room," he explains, "taking an order."

Vivienne waits on the patio, holding onto the wooden railing and kicking at the decking with the heel of her sneaker. She watches a gull dive into the shallows of the bay and pick up a sea urchin. Follows it with her eyes as it catches an updraft and floats to a dizzying height before dropping the urchin onto the rocky beach below. The bird dives to pick at the newly exposed flesh in the cracked shell, and Tama creaks open the screen door. She leans outside, her feet never leaving the ceramic tile of the kitchen. Vivienne turns, the distress on her face plain.

Tama looks behind her. Bradley is standing over a sizzling pan and can't hear what she is saying. "I'll be an hour. Meet you up top."

Vivienne stalks off across the gravel parking lot and heads for the garden of the ruined house, her agitation lending her a frenetic energy, propelling her climb to the top of the hill. The walks Vivienne has been taking to place some distance between herself and Colleen, between herself and Isaiah, have not been like this. They have been aimless, a kind of directionless wandering. She has been sleepwalking about the cove as if the roads are covered in molasses; thick, effortful movement, gravity pulling at her ankles, leaving her exhausted. Peering through windows as she plodded along. Waving at people pulling weeds in their gardens and at women hanging laundry on the line. And they'd waved back at her—from porches and car windows and the wharf and from the other side of the road. Still, she hadn't been able to get any closer than that distant acknowledgement, couldn't find a way to fully interact with anyone. Everything had been glazed over, and she couldn't cut through and touch the real surface of things.

Worse than that, the sight of every beautiful thing—dew-embossed flowers and songbirds and yellow butterflies mating—had tasted sickly sweet. The frosted world felt like sugar crunching between her teeth. She was left feeling sticky and sick and she couldn't quite figure out if it was her that was cloyingly sugar-coated or if she was whole-fleshed and real, wandering about in a marzipan world.

Now she is sucking in air. At the top of the hill, the need to feed her lungs forces her to stop walking and bend over with her hands on her thighs, legs burning. She takes great gulping breaths, she is a glutton for oxygen. Her lungs nearly spastic, she inhales before she has completely exhaled, breaths coming upon her like waves, one crashing into the next. Her skin prickles with heat. She can imagine her face, red as the poppies sprinkled through the grass next to the store in July. As red as the bottom of a boat after you've bled a fish.

The charge up the hill has liberated her. Vivienne has broken through the syrup of numbness she has been drowning in and is taking painful, staggering, bracing breaths. Until she realizes, this isn't true. That isn't what happened. It is not the climb that has jolted her body, and her consciousness, free. It was the moment she stepped over the threshold of the store. The moment she squeezed past Isaiah. Her body touched his and the blister of shock she has been living in burst. She can feel the scalding liquid pouring from it, her lips tasting of salt.

Vivienne stands in the garden of the ruined mansion with its oak trees, listening as her heartbeat slackens, as the space between beats lengthens. It is the first time in days she has felt in her body. She had forgotten physical pain, had forgotten rubbed ankles and blisters. She had forgotten hot, too. She lifts the hem of her T-shirt, a lick of wind cooling her sweaty skin. She had forgotten the bruises on the tenderest skin of her arms, had forgotten that the scabs running like a string of pearls down her spine not only leaked ruby droplets of blood but itched as the skin healed. She longs to rub her back like a bear against one of the rough-barked tree trunks but knows the satisfaction will be temporary and she will re-open every wound.

While she waits, Vivienne walks the stone foundation of the old house, balancing on the rocky outline like a child balancing on a curb. Her feet trace someone else's past, the edges of a disappeared life. She tightropes around the remnants of the foundation, one foot lined up in front of the other, arms outstretched. At first she moves too quickly, she is clumsy and falls into the long grass surrounding—occupying—the house. But her pace slows and her movements become more meditative. Charting the house with her feet becomes less a game, more thoughtful. Isaiah's touch has propelled her up the hill as if she had been caught in the rush of a hurricane, but now she is able to catch her breath. She recognizes she is in the eye of the storm. Her feet trace a path the way her finger followed the outline of the creature in her borrowed book, the way she might trace an escape route on a map.

The easiest thing would be to walk away from the harbour, from the fish, from this summer. She could catch a ride with someone commuting to town, or with the man who drives the Pepsi truck when he drops his weekly delivery at the shop. He'll be here in the morning, Damson Bay is a Monday stop. Still, either of those options means waiting out the night, and if she wants out, she wants out now. She wonders if anyone still hitchhikes. She could stuff her backpack, stick out her thumb, and be in town in a couple of hours. She hears a voice in her head warning her of the dangers—a girl all alone—but surely there are no killers on this sleepy stretch of bay.

Vivienne jumps down from the wall and begins to explore the grassy rooms of the mansion. Instead of furniture there are only places where the chimneys have collapsed, leaving piles of scree to sit on. Instead of wallpaper there are wildflowers: goldenrod and purple fireweed going to feather. An old-fashioned rose growing outside the back stoop has jumped the wall and occupies the kitchen and its rectangular hearth. A dogberry tree has grown up in the place of a lamp, its branches heavy with berries on their way from orange to red.

Vivienne crouches inside, occupying the non-rooms, waiting for the ghosts of rooms past to introduce themselves. She lies back in a patch of yellow grass and sees nothing but sky. Broken stalks poke her skin. She is completely hidden. She imagines the grass growing taller and taller, covering her like a canopy before going to seed. She imagines the chaff dropping onto her stomach and germinating. Grass growing out of her belly, up through her skin, until she is perfectly obscured. Her mind wanders until a decidedly bodily urge calls it back. Vivienne's bladder is full. When she squats in a corner to relieve herself she feels ashamed. What a thing to do. Pee in someone's front room.

Tama finds her sitting on the front stoop, Vivienne's back turned to the spectres sweeping through the house, feigning ignorance as wraiths caress the back of her neck and blow kisses like spider webs into her hair. Tama sits down next to her and runs her hand along the concrete step. The concrete had been mixed by hand using sand carted up the hill from the landwash and is speckled with tiny beach rocks and mussel shells the size of ladybugs.

"There used to be stone figures going up either side of the steps. Like Stations of the Cross. The old skipper that lived here commissioned them. I've seen pictures. Fish and squid and sailing ships. Long gone now. When we were kids you could still find little artefacts, pieces of the statues, in the grass. I found a fin once." She doesn't turn to look at Vivienne but looks out over the water. "But I lost it somewhere along the way."

An army of harried ants scurries across the ground. One trundles behind, lugging the still-twitching corpse of a broken-winged dragonfly. Vivienne and Tama can hear frogs garrumping, their voices thick. An orchestra of plucked rubber bands. Vivienne had not realized how close they are to the boggy highlands she has seen out the truck windows on her trips to Carbonear with Thomas. The house is situated within throwing distance of the marsh, surrounded by flies and the smell of rotting vegetation.

"I'm locked out. They've locked me out. Thrown away the key. Colleen's head just about popped off. She lost her shit over somebody making a call and then I was banished."

"I figured as much." Tama relates the commotion at the café.

"Tama, we have to get her out of here. I can't imagine paying admission to see her in a tank, as an exhibit at an aquarium." Vivienne speaks softly. "Or worse, locked away in a lab. Not able to see her at all, even through glass." Even more softly. "Not knowing what they're doing to her." Vivienne turns to look Tama in the face. "We're out of time, Tama."

"I know."

"They've taken my keys."

At this Tama smiles. "This place was still standing when I was growing up but it was hardly safe. Holes in the floor, holes in the ceiling." Birds nesting in the rafters. The outline of bats against the sky in places the roof had collapsed. "And don't you think the older folks in town didn't try to keep us out of it? Afraid the whole building would cave in on top of us. One little padlock is no match for a pair of bolt cutters."

To the children growing up with Tama, the mansion had been a true haunted house. A place to enter on a dare. To a teenager, a perfect hideout, far enough away from grown-up eyes. Someone had dragged a couple of beat-up lawn chairs into the parlour, and a stack of blue milk crates. There had been parties, and Tama had seen romance in the light of candles glinting off beer bottles, decadence and abandonment floating in the air alongside the smell of weed. Laughter chimed like bells from the girls, like gongs from the boys with their newly changed voices. There were endless kisses and cold fingers under her sweater, hands lingering on her breasts until they warmed.

"This place was a wreck of a house, windows boarded up with sheets of plywood. But there were frescoes painted on the walls inside. Can you imagine?" Tama has floated into the past. "Beautiful, what was left of them. Kids always chipping away at them." And not just kids. There were people around still who had pieces of them, she was sure. "The man who built the house was a ship's captain and he commissioned some Italian painter to do them. The real thing, paint on plaster."

"What were they pictures of?" Vivienne takes Tama's hand.

"Oh, the ocean. Strange islands. Beasts and maidens, ships in stormy seas. Monsters. Every kind of fantastical thing. The story goes that the skipper who built the house was done with the sea. That the day the house was finished his ship unmoored. Drifted out of the harbour on a dead-calm night and wrecked herself on the rocks."

Tama had taken Bradley up here just after they were married but all he'd seen were the rotting planks and the holes where there might be rats and the bird shit. He'd said, you know, those doors are boarded up for a reason. And had refused to go inside.

"It burned maybe ten years ago." A warm spring day, smoke saturating the fog. Grass and alders and raspberry canes had taken right over.

Vivienne and Tama sit on the sun-warmed stone step while the yellow sun drops in the sky, fog rolling in like foamed milk. While they make plans.

"We need to talk to Thomas."

They linger at the ruined mansion with its dusty stories, making plans until the fog starts to roll in and then they wander down the hill to find Thomas at the wharf, shooting the shit on the dock. Vivienne jumps into the punt and busies herself checking gear, making sure there is gas in the motor, in the jerry can tucked in the cuddy. Tama sits on the edge of the dock, swinging her feet. They shout a greeting to him and to the men standing around a cutting table down the length of the wharf. One filleting and three watching, hands in their pockets.

A few minutes later, Thomas saunters over and sits down next to Tama.

"Well, now. What a pair. What are you two criminals up to today?"

Vivienne's heart in her throat. She is a criminal. Or about to be. Or has been ever since she pulled the fish over the side of the gunwale. She is never seasick but the nearly imperceptible motion of the boat, the faint smell of diesel, is making her queasy. The overwhelming sense of having nothing firm beneath her feet making her stomach churn.

Tama speaks first. "Vivienne found something."

"Has she now?"

"She has. She's found something and brought it here, to the cove. She's brought it to the lab."

Thomas looks straight at Vivienne. Her face reddens but she holds his gaze. Tilts her chin at him defiantly.

"Found a little treasure, did she?"

Tama relinquishes a small smile. "She did. But things have gotten more complicated. They're getting ready to move her to St. John's. And that guy knocking around in the blue Honda today is a reporter."

"What do you need?"

He leans forward, arms crossed over his chest.

"A smoke screen, a diversion. All we need you to do is move the truck. Let them think Vivienne has fled the scene with our creature, made a break for town."

"I can do that. Sure that's all you need?"

"Smoke screen. That's you."

Thomas makes a gesture with his hands reminiscent of a bomb going off. Vivienne is dumbfounded, her defiant chin raised in stupefaction. She missteps, the boat still moving beneath her feet, and nearly falls overboard. Thomas reaches for her, his hand solid in hers, as if it is real. She feels the humanness of his hand, the carpals and the phalanges, the sinews and tendons between fingers and thumb and wrist. His grip anchoring her to the world when she would have floated away on a dream of a breeze.

"Watch yourself, Skipper." He looks at Tama, a flicker of amusement sliding across his face. "You didn't tell her? What a sin."

"I thought she had it nine parts figured out."

Vivienne speaks up. "No. I didn't. I don't. I have it no parts figured out." Looking at Tama.

Thomas answers for her. "People have been on the water out here their whole lives. Everyone knows what's in the bay." He has not released her hand. Reminding her she is still here in the world.

"But—" Vivienne's mind whirls like a fishing spool unfurling. "Weren't you going to do something? Weren't you going to try and help her? To stop us?" Her mind flashes to the leaden creature in the tank. "She's not doing so good."

"First," Tama says, "she's sturdier than you might think. Second. We were waiting to see how things played out."

TRUCE

THE most important thing is to keep Ben Sharpe away from the store. Away from the prep table that leads to nowhere, and the computer, and any stray files Colleen and Isaiah may have missed in their clean-up blitzkrieg of the lab. Away from the freezer in the corner that is starting to stink of excrement and rotting food and the kind of sea water that lives under the discharge end of a sewer pipe. Away from its occupant. Away from the smell of effluent and rot. There are places to poke in the store, even if they managed to conceal the freezer, even if they pretend to ignore the smell. There are corners to snoop in.

Colleen imagines Ben Sharpe is nothing like his name, more a Scooby Doo sleuth than a serious investigative reporter. Still, Scooby and Shaggy were nothing if not lucky, and clues fell into their laps. A packing slip or a button. A train ticket or a microscope slide. Colleen refuses to let dumb luck intervene. She is not a gambler. She is not entrusting her fate to the random flip of a card. The deck is stacked and she is still holding aces. Information would be released as she saw fit. When it is most advantageous to her. The house always wins.

The fog dragon that resides just over the far hill has exhaled again. The late afternoon brume rolling into the bay does not fit Colleen's plan. She had hoped to hold the interview with Ben Sharpe on the deck of the staff house but it is getting too wet to sit out. Instead, they will have to make use of the kitchen. While she waits for the clock to find its way to eight o'clock, she collects every scrap of paper, every yellow-lined pad, every data set and pie chart they've printed and poured over, the flurry of plans and secrets Isaiah has strewn from one end of the room to the other. She dumps them into a Tupperware tub. Carries it out to the green truck and lodges it in the space behind the driver's seat. Locks the door. She is sure she has missed nothing. Still, a lingering doubt niggles. Colleen is nothing if not careful and the front verandah would have been preferable. She doesn't want Ben Sharpe to leave with a clue stuck to the bottom of his shoe.

She is pouring the dregs of last night's coffee down the drain when Bradley raps at the glass of the kitchen window with his knuckle. The coffee at the bottom of the pot is thick with grounds, the paper filter in its basket must have ripped. It clings to the side of the stainless steel sink before sliding viscously down the drain. Bradley raises a tray of coffee cups into her line of vision. His expression doleful. He looks as if he hasn't slept. He certainly hasn't shaved. But the coffee wins Colleen over and she pulls on a fleece before joining him outside. The night is warmer than she thought. Bradley turns around and rests the coffee on the glass-topped patio table.

There are two cups in the tray. "One for you. One for the professor."

Colleen eases one from its cardboard grip. "He's not here. He's at the lab." She will hide the other one. Maybe in the microwave. Reheat it later.

"Colleen." Bradley puts out one hand as if approaching an unfamiliar animal. He does not come any closer. "Colleen, I don't know what happened the other night. I thought we were fine."

She takes the lid from the cup. Inhales, searching for notes in the aroma like a wine connoisseur. It smells of warm earth. Oak. Hazelnuts.

"There is no *we* to be fine, Bradley."

The liquid the colour of dark chocolate.

"Is it the professor? He's not what you want. He can't give you what you need."

He could but he won't. Not without some convincing. She takes her first sip. Rolls one small drop around her tongue before swallowing.

"I could care less about Isaiah," is what she says. "Really. This is not about you. Things are complicated with this project. It's become political. It's the only thing I can focus on right now."

"Listen. Just think about it. I'm not done with this thing yet." He pushes himself off the railing to stand in front of her. Colleen is tall but Bradley is taller. They are almost touching. They are close enough that he could dip his head to kiss her but he doesn't. Only the coffee between them. "Think about it." He steps down onto the gravel path leading away from the house and turns to walks backwards, hands in his pockets. "Tama overheard part of a conversation you had this morning. She said you might be looking for a place to have a meeting tonight. Neutral territory. Anyway. She wanted me to let you know you're welcome to use the dining room of the café."

"Did she now?"

"Whatever you were talking about this morning makes her think you're good for business."

In her mind Colleen catalogues the contents of the fridge. Considers the possibility of getting something decent to eat at the café. And neutral territory is just what they need to manage this situation. A space that does not carry a thought of the specimen. A place with no clues to discover.

"Okay. Eight."

Bradley senses her capitulation before she says the word. He turns away, one hand raised in a farewell, before she can see the smile fully open on his face. But she can hear him whistling as he saunters away. Hands in his pockets.

The closed sign is flipped but the lights are on. Colleen and Isaiah head to the back of the dining room, to Colleen's usual table. She pours herself a cup of coffee leaving Isaiah to fend for himself. Bradley pokes his head out of the kitchen. He calls out a greeting and disappears again. Re-emerges a minute later with a plate of quiche tarts. Eggs as yellow as butter, studded through with green and red peppers. Colleen helps herself to two.

"I'll be right through here if you need anything." Bradley disappears into the kitchen, shouting over his shoulder. "Glad for your custom."

"Appreciate you opening for us," says Isaiah gruffly. His voice has lost the magnanimity it carried earlier in the day. His foot taps underneath the table, as if his knee is a piston. Colleen smiles into her lap.

Ben Sharpe is exactly on time. Colleen and Isaiah have just enough time to review their strategy before he strolls into the café.

"Snacks!" He grabs a side plate from the prep station. "And help yourself to coffee, is it?" Colleen and Isaiah have failed to pull a third chair to the table. He steals one from a neighbouring table and sits down with them. Adds three packets of sugar and a glug of cream to his mug.

"These look delicious." In the manner of a growing boy he pops a tart into his mouth. Swallows and says, "I knew you would be civilized about this situation. Like I said earlier, this can be a win-win situation for everybody involved. Let's think of ourselves as partners." He wipes the crumbs from his hands. Lays his phone with its recorder in the middle of the table. "Now. Let's negotiate terms."

Through the open window Colleen can hear a dog bark. Somewhere down the cove, the sound of an engine turning over. Gulls carrying on as a boat pulls into the dock.

CHEKOV

THE green truck sighs to a stop and Thomas pulls the keys from the ignition. Notices, as he closes the door, a clear Tupperware container lodged behind the driver's seat. He pops the lid and flicks through the papers and notebooks stuffed inside. Tucks it under his arm before he heads down the road.

"Little foggy!" The fishermen on the wharf call out to Vivienne. "Watch yourself out there tonight. It'll be easy enough to get turned around if you're not paying attention."

Vivienne unlashes the painter, throws it into the prow. "I will be." She pulls the punt close and lowers herself into it, hauls at the ripcord to start the outboard. Panic or antici-pation or adrenalin has made her strong, the tension in her body translating as physical strength, and the motor starts on the first pull. She waves to the fishermen as she eases away from the berth.

It is easy to tell they are past the height of summer. Eight o'clock in the evening and a hint of dusk is already settling like down. The air is damp, the sea dead calm. The doldrums. A fate worse than a summer hurricane any sailor would tell you. At least a storm is something you can dance with, something you can fight. In the doldrums there is nothing to be done but float and wait. Still, the sky suggests it is willing to clear. The weather has not yet decided what it's going to be.

She eases the boat across the bay, motoring slowly, hoping to make the growl of the outboard as inconspicuous as possible. In the foggy air, sound is magnified, sound travels. Five minutes later she is a stone's throw from the back of the store. She cuts the engine and lets the boat drift on the tide, mindful of the rocks beneath the hull. It is not easy to land this close on the shore. She can imagine the proper pier the store once boasted. Long and skinny, extending like a finger—a reverse fjord—into the water.

Vivienne grabs the grappling hook, and uses it to snare a barnacle-encrusted rock. She pulls the boat as close as she can to the back bridge before flipping the hook over and poling towards shore like a Venetian gondolier. The back end of the boat drifts forwards, bringing her broadside to the landwash. She hears the scrape of keel on rock. The paint-peeled wall of the store looms above her, the dilapidated deck a mouthful of haphazard teeth. She is using all her strength to hold the boat steady, the rough wood of the hook chafing her hands. A figure steps out of the shadows.

Tama reaches out to hold the boat steady and Vivienne scrambles over the side and into the water. She is wearing shorts and sneakers, rather than rubber boots, erring on the side of flight. The water is frigid against her skin, a shock of cold between her toes, in the crooks of her knees. The salt stinging old wounds. Silently, efficiently, the two women secure the boat to the rotting deck post. It continues to drift towards shore on the tide. A hollow knocking as it bumps against the rocks. It will hold long enough. They are lucky the night is so calm.

"Did Thomas get away alright?" Vivienne speaks first.

"He did. He texted me as he was leaving. He's got the truck tucked in behind the staff house. You won't be able to see it from the road. Not unless you're really looking."

Vivienne bends to pick up a beach rock the size and shape of an orange, smooth and round. She heaves herself onto the deck, feeling how the softened wood gives under the weight of her body. Puts the rock down long enough to peel off her sodden sneakers and throw them to one side, weighing it in her hand as she retrieves it. The stone is solid, heavy in her cupped palm.

"He said it was easy as pie. No trouble at all. He waited until they were inside a few minutes and then opened the front door and popped the clutch." Tama laughs. "Good god, that truck. She is so loud. He let her roll all the way down the hill before he chanced turning her on."

Vivienne stands up, rock in hand. The boat secured, she and Tama creep around to the front of the store. Colleen and Isaiah are meeting with the reporter, and they figure they have the best part of an hour before the truck is discovered missing. Still, it seems best to cling to the shadows and keep their voices low. Tama is as proficient with the bolt cutters as advertised. The blades slice through the leg of the padlock in one snip. They slip it from its loop and ease through the door, closing it softly behind them, as though Colleen and Isaiah might hear them from the café. As if their voices might carry that far on the fog. Vivienne takes the second padlock, the one looped on the hook inside the door—their state-of-the-art security system—and slips it into her pocket. They don't intend to be here long enough to need it.

They head straight for the fish. She has sunk to the bottom of the tank. The water that had been murky the last time the women had been here has taken on an algaeic green glow. Vivienne and Colleen have rigged a filter to circulate clean seawater through the tank and Vivienne had cleaned the lines twice a day to keep them from clogging, but the filter is meant for a regular household tank. It is meant for goldfish, and it cannot keep up, gurgling hopelessly in the corner. Sand has made it into the freezer through the intake hose, and a smattering of glowing phytoplankton. The plankton float on the surface of the water like stars peeking through a break in the clouds. A single constellation. The creature is curled like a new fern on the floor of the freezer. A week at the bottom of a well.

Vivienne reaches in as far as she can, stretching her fingers to touch her, her feet leaving the floor. The fish makes no movement towards Vivienne's hand. "We might have to dive in after her."

"You're already wet," Tama points out. Vivienne pulls her arm out of the tank. For the space of a long breath they watch the fish sleep.

"The orange-shaped rock is still in Vivienne's hand. She lays it on the workbench and looks around, her hands on her hips.

"We're going to need a couple of buckets, the bailer's not going to cut it. And the fish boxes are over there." She is thinking out loud. "It's going to have to be the fish box again. It's the only thing I think we'll fit her in. We can carry her one to a side."

As Tama collects supplies, Vivienne strips a trove of sample-filled containers of their contents. Microscope slides, and vials of blood. Test tubes filled with scale scrapings, glistening shards of peridot and gold. Pink plugs of flesh packed in bags of beer cooler ice. "I am so sorry about that," she whispers. Packs almost everything into the corner of the fish box Tama has pulled out of the corner. A collection of treasure to be buried at sea.

The box of microscope slides, filed as neatly as books on a shelf, she takes to the workbench. She lays them out just as neatly on the worn wooden surface. The burnished rock fits perfectly within the curve of her hand and with her rock Vivienne smashes each slide. Pushing down on them, pulverizing them, until only a field of splinters and glass dust remains. She finds a brush and sweeps the glittering pile into a dustpan and dumps them into the belly of the woodstove. Stirs them into the pile of cold ash.

At the café, Ben Sharpe is tabling the topic of credible evidence. They have gotten past the preliminaries and are discussing details. Exclusive access and first rights of publication and word counts and photos. The names in the captions. Colleen says, "I have some things in the truck that might help. I'll be right back."

The two women stand in the middle of the floor, hands on their hips like superheroes. Vivienne tries to take in everything, to stamp it on her brain. The smell of coarse salt infusing the wooden frame of the store, and the walls, from a century of salting fish. The smell of motor oil, of small tools and boat motors. The smell of rubbing alcohol and the smell of the sea, the stench of rotting capelin, and the putrid aroma emanating from the corner. She tries to memorize the light through the window and the creak of the walls as they collapse, slowly, into the landwash. She misses the muffled sound of gulls. The fog has lulled them to sleep, they are bobbing, dreaming, on the quiet sea.

Tama speaks into the silence. "I think that's everything."

A deep sigh from Vivienne. "Alright. Let's get things moving."

Colleen walks out the front door of the café. She is down the steps and across the parking lot before she realizes it is empty of any vehicle apart from Ben Sharpe's Honda, parked haphazardly at an angle. She circles in place, wondering if she's missed it, if she's parked the green truck somewhere else and has somehow forgotten. She ventures another two steps forward, checking to see if the truck has crouched down behind the blue Honda, if it is playing hide and seek, if she can catch it peeking out. It is nowhere to be seen. Colleen is momentarily mystified. It's not as if the truck could hide. Who could have taken it? Only Vivienne but Vivienne can't drive stick. A second later and anger boils up thick as tar. That fucking Thomas. And she is thundering up the stairs, shouting as she goes.

Vivienne and Tama peer into the white freezer. Vivienne stands on a cardboard box that cannot quite support her weight, reaching into the murky water. The filter is in the way. She shuts it off and removes it and all its tubing, and it feels as if she is removing life support. She reaches in to touch the fish, running the tip of her finger along her fluke. Flesh rippling at her touch. Tama on standby waiting for direction. The box giving a little underfoot.

"Hold on."

She pushes away the treacherous box and grabs a lab stool from the workbench. Climbs up to kneel on top of it, the metal rim digging into her kneecaps as she leans forward. She plunges both arms in then straightens up, soaking wet. Her shirt dripping water.

"This is ridiculous." She strips to her sports bra and reaches as far as she can into the tank, her back the shape of a willow leaning over a slow-moving river. From here she can put her hands on either side of the fish's tail but cannot find enough leverage to pull her upwards.

"I'm going to have to get in and try and lift her out. Move that fish box right over close. Be ready to hoist."

Vivienne swings her feet over the edge. She holds herself aloft on the rim, trying to place her feet without stepping on the fish, and slips into the tank. The water is shockingly cold and dirty. Bits of organic material float through the water, brushing against her legs like lily pads in a pond, weeds threatening to entangle her legs and drown her.

"Vivienne." The word like the peal of a bell. Vivienne looks over her shoulder, startled, at the note in Tama's voice. Tama's head is tilted to one side, she is studying Vivienne's back. She reaches over and traces an invisible line parallel to Vivienne's spine, contemplating the angry violet bruises, the delicate scabs, ready to break open at the slightest caress. The weight of her finger as gentle as a whisper of smoke.

Vivienne returns her attention to her feet. "Later. We can talk about that later." Solid footing is elusive but she settles on a position, tries to ground her feet on the slippery floor of the freezer.

"You ready?"

Vivienne nods. She takes a breath and submerges her head beneath the surface of the water. Tries to open her eyes but the salt and effluent sting so sharply she is forced to squeeze them shut again. Sightless, she bends down and grasps the fish in two hands, pulls her towards the surface. And then, with a twist of her neck and a weak snap, the fish is swimming free of Vivienne's grasp. Vivienne draws her hand back sharply and surfaces, blinking open her stinging eyes to assess the puncture wound in her wrist. The creature has bitten her. The next stage of Tama's mission is going to involve Polysporin.

"She's not quite the convalescent we took her for." Tama is staring into the tank.

"She is not."

Vivienne can feel the muscles of the creature's fluke twitch as they brush against her, as she begins to circle. Not the furious figure eights of the first days of her imprisonment, but a lazy loop around Vivienne's torso and legs. Vivienne can feel the buds of new scales scrape the skin of her thighs, etching fine lines in her flesh as she passes. She feels as though she is in the middle of a slowly intensifying whirlpool. The eddy growing stronger with each turn of the fish's body.

"What has she done? Made a run for town?" Colleen narrows her eyes. "Trying to find a ride back into St. John's. Jesus fool. She must have that Thomas convinced to bring her as far as Carbonear or some idiot thing." She taps her finger on the tabletop, thinking.

Ben Sharpe answers her. "How much gas is in the tank? I bet they have to stop at the gas station up on the high road before they make the run in." He looks at his watch. "They can't be gone any longer than fifteen minutes." He is fishing his keys from his pocket.

"The tank is licking empty. If you're lucky you'll catch them." She watches him jog out the door. Turns to Isaiah. "Go and keep an eye on him. I don't want him getting any ideas about grabbing an exclusive and making a run for the hills, either." Isaiah hurries after, seeing, no doubt, an opportunity to get Ben Sharpe alone for a few minutes.

Colleen waits until the car is up the hill and out of sight before pushing her way through the swinging door and striding into the kitchen. Bradley is standing at the counter, a glass raised to his lips. A bottle of wine is open on the counter, a second glass sitting next to it.

"I need a ride," Colleen says. "I need to check on something at the lab."

***

Vivienne leans her weight into the creature, pinning her to the side of the freezer. She can feel the creature's flesh quivering against her legs. Her own flesh is nearly numb with cold.

"Let's make this quick."

She forms a basket with her hands, as if she is boosting someone over a fence. The cold is making her clumsy, her knitted fingers feel thick. She positions the pinned fish as best she can against her body, and with a heave, pushes the creature, and a fan of water, over the rim of the tank. The fish spills into the fish box, Tama directing her fall. It is not a soft landing. The seaweed arms come last. Vivienne is put in mind of an octopus sliding off a table. A long-tentacled thing that even in death seems alive. The seaweed appendages attach to the side of the freezer the way wet hair lacquers a cheek in the rain. The fish is mostly in the box. Tama gathers stray kelp like a little girl gathering flowers.

"Okay. A handle each now." Vivienne pulls herself out of the freezer and she and Tama lift the box from the floor. It is heavy, its heaviness compounded by the restless movements of the fish inside. Vivienne is streaming water. They carry the box across the floor, urgency upon them like a fast-breathing animal and Vivienne, shivering in the night air, starts to giggle. The absurdity of it. Her arms turn to jelly.

"Hold on a second." She drops the box to the floor with a thud. Her arm jerking at the shoulder socket. "I'm so sorry. Hang on." A wave of laughter threatens to completely overtake her. She is bent over at the waist, eyes leaking, stomach aching.

Tama gives a small laugh, too, though it doesn't count for much. Waits for the crest of the wave to pass. "Are you okay?"

"I am. It's just—" Vivienne takes a shaky inhalation. "It's just all so ridiculous."

They hoist again and start their shuffling dance towards the door.

Vivienne and Tama are mismatched dance partners. Tama is taller than Vivienne, and stronger, and the fish box lists as the women carry it to the door. The fish, and the weight of their cargo, slides towards Vivienne. They set it down every ten feet and Vivienne catches her breath before they hoist it again, shuffling forward, her side of the box inches from the floor. The muscles of Vivienne's shoulders are liquefying. She is afraid they will turn to water before they finish their task. She is afraid she will not make it. Her fingers are cramping, turning white at the knuckles.

They reach the doorway and peek outside. In the yard, nothing moves. They might be looking at a film set rather than the real thing. There are no ripples on the muddy puddles, no disturbances in the air. The grass does not move, or the gravel. No gull cries, they can hear no quads on the hill, no voices. No footsteps. They ease open the door and venture outside. Nothing jumps from behind a rock to surprise them. There is no ambush. They heave the box again and hustle it around the corner and out of sight, a waddling two-step, the creature sloshing back and forth in the plastic container. They set it down while Tama doubles back around the corner to close the door, to hook the padlock over its metal loop, to make away with her bolt cutters. To make it look, at least from a distance, that the door is barred shut.

Vivienne heaves. The fish slides in a slippery, fleshy pile to the far end of the box as she pulls it along the wooden deck, hitting each plank like a stick run along a picket fence. Xylophoning and loud. The sound seems to echo and Vivienne realizes there are in fact two sounds, the bump, bump, bump of the box and a rumble that she recognizes as the sound of a car engine. She listens as it turns into the gravel lane and pulls into the driveway that leads to the store. The driver kills the engine.

Tama is fumbling with the lock when she hears a car in the lane. She can see it flash in the gaps between the houses like still frames from a movie, and she knows she is caught. It is her own car. It is pulling into the driveway. She takes one step away from the deck on the side of the store. The sickly sweet smell of exhaust filling her nostrils. Bradley is behind the wheel. Their eyes meet through the windshield and something tight between them starts to unwind. A not-so-secret secret unravelling in front of them.

Colleen struggles with her seatbelt. She flings it aside as she bursts through the passenger side door and it hits the side of the car with a metallic thwack. A ghost of a smile dances across Tama's lips and her heart warms for Bradley—one degree. Him and the seatbelts. He wouldn't leave the driveway without insisting Colleen buckle up, wouldn't start the engine. He'd bought she and Vivienne fifteen seconds while he waited stubbornly for the click of Colleen's seatbelt. Such a cautious driver. He would have stopped at the bottom of the driveway for a good look either way, too, even if nothing was coming. He would have made a complete stop at the stop sign at the bottom of the hill.

Thomas is waiting for Vivienne at the rear of the store. He slides around the corner to help her with the fish box, both of them freezing at the sound of the approaching vehicle. Listening as the driver shuts off the motor and someone steps bellowing from the car. Wordlessly they take a handle each and carry the creature to the edge of the bridge, no breaks, no resting tired biceps. The panic making Vivienne strong. There are voices inside the store, now, and through the thin walls they can hear Colleen, it is without a doubt Colleen, and she is shouting. Where is it? Where is it? There is crashing inside, the sound of something being thrown and then a repeated hammering, like a mallet hitting a spike.

Thomas is in the water, pulling the punt close while Vivienne scrambles over the side and into the boat, banging her thigh against the oarlock in her haste. A bruise collected for later. Vivienne braces her legs, locking her knees around one of the wooden thwarts. Thomas is scrambling, too, trying to keep the boat steady and handle the fish box at the same time. They have lost their third hand. They are trying not to move too quickly, trying not to make mistakes, trying not to make any noise.

It is Vivienne who solves their problem. She clambers back over the gunwale and scoots until she is sitting on the very edge of the weather-softened dock. Hooks her legs over the side of the boat and pulls it close with her feet. Thomas hops on the deck and drags the box onto the edge of the boat and together they wrestle it into the bottom of the punt. They have left the five-gallon buckets Tama had gathered inside the door and there is no going back for them. Instead they use the bailer to slosh a couple inches of water into the box. Vivienne reaches in and repositions the fish, trying to move her gills as far into the skim of water as she can. She runs her hand along the fish's fluke. Straightens her tail like a bridesmaid straightening a veil. A second car pulls into the driveway. Thomas scoops faster. They'll need at least a couple of inches if they want the fish to survive the trip.

"What the fuck are you doing here?" The full force of Colleen's anger is directed at Tama. Her words are like nails, like shrapnel in a dirty homemade bomb. "Where's Vivienne? Where is she?" And then, noticing the padlock dangling from Tama's fingers, "Were you inside? What the fuck were you doing in there?"

Tama stands her ground. She is not intimidated by Colleen's bluster, she is impervious to her red hot words. She is standing in front of the door but takes a polite step to one side as Colleen barrels towards her. Calm in the face of Colleen's anger. Colleen storms inside and heads straight for the tank. Knuckles white, cords popping from her neck.

"She's gone." Colleen looks at Tama and then back at the freezer. "Where is she?" Her voice hissingly quiet.

In answer, Tama quietly closes the door, obliterating Colleen's face from view. Plants her feet and sets her legs, locking them into place. Something smashes against the door. She feels it reverberate through her spine. She braces herself and is ready when Colleen makes her first run at the door. Bradley watching the entire exchange from where he stands beside the fender of the car, bewildered.

She speaks to him for the first time. "Help me."

And he does, pushing a shoulder into the door. A blue Honda is on its way down the lane.

The blue Honda is Ben Sharpe's. Ben Sharpe is driving, Isaiah in the passenger seat next to him. The car takes the corner into the yard sharply, sliding a little on the loose gravel. An orange cat bursts from the yellow grass and Ben Sharpe screeches to a stop, narrowly missing it. The cat stands its ground, arching its back and hissing. The day is beginning to fade to twilight and in the approaching dusk sparks of static electricity jumping from its titian fur like flankers. Isaiah steps from the passenger seat, talking before he is out of the car and the cat dances back into the cover of the grass.

"Is she here?" He is looking at Bradley. "Ben noticed you headed down as we headed up." Something crashes against the closed door. It sounds as if Colleen has picked up some heavy item, a cinder block or the prostrate door to nowhere or a boat motor, and is using it as a battering ram. The wooden planks jolt against Tama's back.

At the sound, Isaiah stops chattering. His face darkens. He lowers his voice, as if he is trying to embody thunder. "I'd like to get in there, I think. Into the lab." He is definite. "Move out of the way."

Tama stares him down and then steps out of the way, pulling Bradley along with her. She is tempted to try and time Colleen's barrage of the door with the moment Isaiah flings it open. Instead, she steps to the side in the space between charges. Colleen is spotlighted, a bull ready to charge. The surprise of the door opening causes her to check her movement and she stumbles. She cannot see who is silhouetted in the doorway.

"Where did you put her?" She is roaring now.

Isaiah answers. "Is Vivienne here?" He steps inside the building.

"The sample. She's taken the goddamn sample."

Behind the store, someone is attempting to start an outboard motor. Tama launches herself from the stoop, Colleen at her heels, pushing Isaiah out of the way as she passes. Isaiah doubles back to grab something off the plastic-covered table that leads to nowhere and chases after her.

"Take your time. You don't want to flood her," Thomas says after Vivienne has jerked on the ripcord for a second time. He is standing on the bridge, seawater pouring from his clothes, trying to release the painter from the wooden deck post. The railing is rotting, slowly collapsing into the sea, and a space has opened up between the railing and the post. The rope is caught in the gap. Thomas is struggling to pull it free when Tama rounds the corner, shouting.

"Go! You're out of time."

Vivienne yanks the ripcord. The engine catches with a roar. She eases the boat into the bay as far as the rope will allow. Isaiah is on top of them. He is carrying the dart gun in his hand. The boat still tethered to land.

"Stop!" He is screaming. The boat is out of reach. He points the gun at Vivienne. She fishes under the cuddy for a filleting knife and while Isaiah screams she sets to work, hacking at the rope, at this last thing holding her to shore. Isaiah is waving the gun in his hand, jabbering mindlessly. She is not listening to what he is saying. She can barely hear him. It is gibberish, meaningless sound. The back deck seems suddenly crowded, and she wonders briefly if it will hold the weight of all the people collected there, but she focuses on no one, they are a single entity, an amorphous body. Her world is the rope and the knife. She saws through the fibres, one by one, and then, with a last slash of the knife, the boat floats free. She looks up to see Isaiah jump into the water. He has the dart gun above his head and is wading towards her. She thinks he will try and swim for her. She reaches behind her to open the throttle.

Despite everything, the blast is unexpected, the dart upon her before she can even think to evade it. It buries itself in the muscle of her thigh, the pain searing and sudden, the dart like a feathered arrow shot from a bow. It performs its job faultlessly, biting into her leg and stealing a tissue sample before losing its grip and slipping to the floor of the boat. She retrieves it from where it has fallen and throws it overboard for Isaiah to reel in, bringing with it its prize of skin and flesh. Leaving the rest of her intact.

SUNSET

THE pain of the dart is searing. Vivienne presses her hand to her thigh, trying to stop the gush of blood. She stuffs her fist against the wound and looks back once as she leaves the cove. Stick figures populate the bridge at the back of the store. Colleen stomps from one end of the deck to the other, a stiff-legged tin soldier. She twists to shout at Vivienne at each turn, her words lost before they reach her; the distance and the sound of the outboard rendering all the actors mute. Tama and Bradley stand near each other, not quite touching. Tama waves like a mechanical doll. Thomas clings to the deck post like a monkey holding fast to the rigging of a sailing ship, to the mast, swinging his whole arm in her direction. Ben Sharpe is in the corner, taking pictures of a girl in a boat.

Isaiah is nearly invisible. He is in the centre of the frame, chest deep in water, motionless. Vivienne wonders if he will ever move. She rounds the point, and the scene behind her disappears. She wonders how long it will take him to dissolve.

Rags of mist litter the bay but the fog is lifting. Daylight slipping away like water in a sieve, as if night is in a hurry to arrive. The sunset is sudden and spectacular. Red sky at night. Vivienne recites the rhyme like a mantra, like a prayer. A bird, late coming home, floats on a draft high in the sky. Gliding. Effortless.

Vivienne can feel the air on her face, and she can taste brine on her lips. She can feel the vibration of the engine, in the hand holding the tiller, and up into her arm. She feels solid. As if she exists. She is as definite as a shoal beneath the surface of the changeable ocean. As real as an island reaching into an ephemeral sky.

She takes the boat farther into open water. Follows the line of hills and cliffs, past the beacon and its reaching light, past the ship that wandered off to sink. She opens the throttle and lets the boat fly, salt spray misting her face and her hair. Down the shore, she pulls into a crevice in the rock face. The surface of the sea throbs, luminous and blue. Somewhere beneath the keel, a garden of kelp and sea fans wave. Crabs hide behind rocky outcrops and mussels open their shells to peek out. Sea stars tumble along the sea floor.

The fissure in the escarpment opens to reveal a tiny rocky beach, inaccessible from above. She cuts the engine and lets the boat drift. The punt catches a swell and Vivienne undulates to its rhythm while the silence flooding her ears dissolves into the sound of pebbles caught in the quiet waves. She sits on the plank seat until her pulse echoes the tide, until her breath repeats the murmur of the breeze on the water, until her heart breathes the wind and her lungs beat with the rhythm of the sea. For now, the ghosts of fear and loneliness, of pain and self-doubt evaporate. The wraiths of lover's kisses and quarrels vanish into nothingness. Grabbing fingers dissipate like smoke.

The creature is spiralled in the bottom of the plastic fish box like a nautilus shell, like a galaxy. Vivienne's hips sway as she stands and reaches to gather her up, the fish's face against her shoulder. She can feel the creature's muscles quiver, she can feel her heart beating against her own.

Vivienne braces herself against the side of the boat and lowers her fish into the sea. Ribbons of kelp slip between her fingers and the creature sinks below the surface, out of sight. The still, dark night settles on her skin. The air is warm. The sea aglow. A coppery fluke disturbs the floating constellations, scattering them like handfuls of stars.

ACKNOWLEDGEMENTS

Thanks are extended to everyone at Breakwater Books, especially James Langer.

This book was completed in partial fulfillment of the Masters of Arts program at Memorial University of Newfoundland and Labrador. Thanks are extended to the staff and faculty of the Department of English, especially Jennifer Lokash, Rob Finley, Danine Farquharson, and Maureen Battcock. Your support was appreciated more than you know.

Thank you to Paula Mendonça for reading the manuscript and offering such helpful advice on the world of fishes and scientific research. *Muito obrigado.*

A monstrous thank you to the lovely, brilliant, and wildly generous Lisa Moore. You have been a wonderful mentor, my chief cheerleader, and a true friend. I have loved working with you.